Murder Under A British Moon

A Mona Moon Mystery
Book Nine

Abigail Keam

Worker Bee Press

Special thanks to Liz Hobson and Jesse Coffey.

Edited by Baker Blooper Editing.

ISBN 978 1 953478 09 2
62122

Published in the USA by

Worker Bee Press
P.O. Box 485
Nicholasville, KY 40340

Books By Abigail Keam

Josiah Reynolds Mysteries
Death By A HoneyBee I
Death By Drowning II
Death By Bridle III
Death By Bourbon IV
Death By Lotto V
Death By Chocolate VI
Death By Haunting VII
Death By Derby VIII
Death By Design IX
Death By Malice X
Death By Drama XI
Death By Stalking XII
Death By Deceit XIII
Death By Magic XIV
Death By Shock XV
Death By Chance XVI
Death By Poison XVII

The Mona Moon Mystery Series
Murder Under A Blue Moon I
Murder Under A Blood Moon II
Murder Under A Bad Moon III
Murder Under A Silver Moon IV
Murder Under A Wolf Moon V
Murder Under A Black Moon VI
Murder Under A Full Moon VII
Murder Under A New Moon VIII
Murder Under A British Moon IX
Murder Under A Bridal Moon X

Last Chance For Love Romance Series
Last Chance Motel I
Gasping For Air II
The Siren's Call III
Hard Landing IV
The Mermaid's Carol V

PROLOGUE

He spoke English, French, German, Italian, Polish, and Hindi like a native. Because his features were bland, he could blend in anywhere and not be noticed. He had bribed contacts at Brynelleth and secreted a way into the ancient manor without being detected. As an SS agent from Sicherheitsdienst, he had been ordered to persuade, coerce, threaten, or blackmail Mona Moon into signing copper contracts with the Third Reich. If not, he was to *neutralize* her. Maybe a new head of Moon Enterprises would be more amenable to their needs. The Germans needed vast amounts of the ore for their weapons rearmament. After all, they had a world to conquer.

1

Mona, Robert, and Violet stood on the deck as the steamship was docking in Plymouth, southwest England. A crowd stood on the pier waving handkerchiefs as the ship's passengers threw confetti and streamers on those below in a gasp of welcoming exhilaration.

Excited, Violet grasped Mona's hand. "Oh, Miss, I can't believe we are in Great Britain again and going to see Brynelleth. I'm shivering with anticipation."

"I hope it lives up to your expectation, Violet," Robert said. "You may be disappointed."

"Oh, it will. It will."

Smiling at Violet's enthusiasm, Robert turned to Mona. "I'm going to get our trunks ready, darling. I shan't be long." He gave her a quick kiss on the cheek.

Mona, a little more circumspect, scanned the crowd below and spotted Mr. Dankworth and Mr. Madgwick, solicitors for the Brynelleth estate. Her heart sank, but she maintained a composed appearance, as she didn't want to distract from Violet's joy. Dankworth and Madgwick had previously traveled to Kentucky and tried to coerce Mona into signing onerous agreements binding her and any possible offspring she and Robert may produce. Mona refused to sign the contracts and sent the lawyers skedaddling back to Brynelleth with their tails tucked between their legs.

The SS Statendam came to a jerky halt against the pier jostling the topside passengers. Mona and Violet grabbed hold of the banister and steadied themselves while the ship came to a complete stop.

"Are you ladies all right?"

Mona and Violet turned to face a suave, handsome German businessman whom they had met while dining at Captain Bigl's table. Mona answered, "We are fine. Thank you for asking, Herr Ribbentrop."

"May I escort you from the ship, Fraulein Moon?"

Not wanting to insult her new acquaintance, Mona carefully replied, "That is very gallant of you, sir, but my fiancé will be along shortly. He went in search of a porter to help with our trunks."

"Very well, then. I hope to see you charming ladies in the future." He pulled out his wallet. "Here is my card. I will be staying at the Savoy if you ever need my assistance while you are in London."

Mona nodded graciously and took the card.

"We're staying at the Savoy as well," Violet piped up.

Mona's heart sank at Violet's revelation. She had learned from President Roosevelt's spy master, William Donovan, to beware of strangers who tried to ingratiate themselves. After her experience with German spies in Washington early this year, Mona understood why the rich and the powerful were often standoffish with outsiders. It might not be because they were rude or arrogant. It might be due to the fact they needed to be vigilant, especially since events were heating up in Europe. Ribbentrop asked too many questions, was too slick with his genteel manners, and was German. His eyes smoldered, looking like he had swallowed the canary and had to restrain himself from licking his lips.

Oh, Lordy, Robert couldn't stand him, and it was all he could do to be polite to the man.

"Then perhaps we might have dinner together during your stay?"

Mona smiled graciously. "It would be our pleasure, but I'm afraid we'll be staying only one night before travelling to our destination."

"And that will be Brynelleth?" Ribbentrop inquired.

Mona didn't respond.

Ignoring Mona's hesitation, he said, "I understand it is a beautiful estate. I, myself, will be venturing to the English countryside to a party at the estate of Lady Furness."

Mona extended her hand. "I hope you enjoy your holiday, Herr Ribbentrop."

"Ladies, I bid you adieu." Ribbentrop kissed Mona's hand and bowed before turning to exit the ship.

Mona sighed with relief.

Violet studied Mona's face and asked, "Why don't you like him?"

"You know the expression 'a wolf in sheep's clothing?'"

"Yes."

"You just saw the human version of it."

"I guess I shouldn't have told him that we were staying at the Savoy."

"No, Violet, you shouldn't have. I doubt the man is staying at the Savoy. He was just trying to see where we were staying, so he took a stab in the dark."

Violet's eyes widened. "Have I put us in danger?"

"I don't know except that we seem to have drawn that man's attention for some reason. He was always hovering around us like a duck on a Junebug during the voyage. The less we say about our business, the better."

"I'm sorry. I know we had a talk about this before we left Kentucky."

"Yes, we did. Please take heed. Remember when Lady Alice Morrell Nithercott was kidnapped. We must take precautions."

Tears formed in Violet's eyes.

"Oh, none of that, Violet. Best foot forward. If this is the worst mistake you make in life, then you and Saint Peter will be greeting the rest of us miscreants at the pearly gates. Dry your eyes, now. Here comes Robert."

Lawrence Robert Emerton Dagobert Farley, Duke of Brynelleth, walked jauntily toward the two women. Holding out luggage tickets, he said, "I got our trunks taken care of. They'll be waiting for us on the dockside."

Mona motioned to the crowd. "Mr. Dankworth and Mr. Madgwick are down below."

Robert leaned over the rail. "What in the blazes are they doing here? I gave instructions that we were not to be met."

"If they are here with some new contract for me to sign, I won't," Mona said, emphatically.

"Don't worry, darling," Robert said. "I'll take care of them." He placed his hands on the small of both women's backs. "Come, ladies, let me escort you off this tin can."

Violet giggled.

Mona took a deep breath. She had no idea what awaited her, but she was anxious to see Brynelleth. She was plunging a lot of money into the estate and wanted to see what she was getting for her investment. Mona crooked her arm around Robert's. "I'm game if you are."

"Chin up, eyes straight ahead, and best foot forward, m'ladies. Let's disembark," Robert coaxed.

Mona smiled and let Robert guide her through the throng of people waiting to go ashore. "Violet, hold on to my dress, so you don't lose us."

"I'm right behind you, Miss Mona. Don't worry about me. I'm a big girl."

Mona bit her lip as she was jostled by those rushing down the gangway. She looked behind her for reassurance that the girl was in step behind them. Mona knew she was being overprotective with Violet, but had promised Violet's mother to take care of her. Violet was a young woman now, and not a child, but still, it was difficult for Mona not to smother Violet. She felt very motherly toward her.

Violet smiled back and wiggled her way to the other side of Robert. Suddenly, Robert put his arm around Violet and pulled her out of the way of an upstart young man barging in the opposite direction of the crowd on the gangplank. Holding onto her hat, Violet declared, "Goodness. How rude. That man almost knocked me into the water. Couldn't he have waited to board until everyone had departed?"

Mona didn't reply as they were nearing the dock. She spied photographers surrounding those arriving and taking pictures.

Feeling Mona stiffen, Robert whispered, "Steady, old girl, smile and be gracious. This type of thing goes with the territory. After all, an English duke arriving from the States is news for the boys from Fleet Street."

Two of the six Pinkertons, traveling incognito as Mona's bodyguards, casually blocked the photographers from getting too close to the couple.

Surprised, Robert glanced at Mona. He knew a Pinkerton interception move when he saw one and wondered how he had never noticed the bodyguards on the ship. "Are these your men?"

"Yes, I felt I needed them as there has been a rash of abductions in Europe." Mona didn't tell Robert that she had been receiving death threats in the mail for several weeks now, warning her not to come. Some of the letters had been postmarked from Great Britain. It seemed that a few of the King's loyal subjects were against the new Duke of Brynelleth marrying an American.

"But that has been on the continent. Not England."

"Oh, that's right. England doesn't have any crime," Mona replied, jokingly. "Come on. Let's see what Dankworth wants."

The three stood off to the side as Dankwork and Madgwick approached them. The men doffed their hats and gave a short bow. "Your Grace. Miss Moon." They nodded to Violet.

"What the devil are you men doing here?" asked Robert, perturbed. "I gave instructions that we were not to be met in London."

Giving an apologetic cough, Dankworth said, "Yes, Your Grace. We know, Your Grace, but we have a slight problem at Brynelleth of which we wanted to make you aware."

Robert was alarmed. "It's not a fire, is it?" Robert dreaded a fire at Brynelleth most of all.

Madgwick cast a glance at Dankworth. "No, sir. It's the Polish workers whom Miss Moon hired. They have gone on strike. Very little has been done, I'm afraid."

"Is that all?" Mona sighed with relief, but she was aware of the solicitors' subtle dig. As she was used to handling employee complaints, Mona asked, "What are their grievances?"

"It's hard to understand as they don't speak proper English," Dankworth said.

"What happened to the foreman I hired? He speaks English."

"We think he's the one stirring up the workers."

Mona understood already what was happening at Brynelleth. "I see. Tell the workers I will settle their disputes when I arrive at Brynelleth. They were hired by me, so I'll handle the situation. His Grace will not need to be involved."

Both solicitors gave a glance at Robert, questioning Mona's statement. "When will that be?" Mr. Dankwork finally asked, pushing up his pince-nez.

Robert answered, "We will be staying in London overnight. The ladies need a rest. We should be expected before lunch tomorrow."

"But Your Grace?" Dankworth said.

"Excuse me. Is there running water at

Brynelleth?" Mona asked.

"Of course, Miss."

"Do the bathrooms work?"

"Yes, Miss." The two solicitors glanced at each other. "Some of them do."

"Is the electricity working?"

"Somewhat."

"Then we shall be fine. Until then, the house staff is expected to clean what they can. The gardeners tidy up what they can, and the hired laborers continue with their tasks. If they don't, I will fire everyone when I arrive with no pay, and there will be no letters of reference. Is that understood?"

Dankworth pleaded with Robert. "Your Grace?"

"It's Miss Moon's money that is funding the renovation of Brynelleth, which will benefit the entire community. Let's try to work with her, shall we, lads?"

"Yes, Your Grace." Both solicitors bowed in deference.

"Good men. See you at Brynelleth. Chin chin," Robert said. "Ladies, let's gather our trunks and be off." Before heading to the Savoy,

Mona and Robert decided to pose for the photographers and answer questions from the reporters.

"Your Grace, it is rumored that you are already secretly married to Miss Mona Moon."

"Is that a fact or a question?" Robert shot back, good-naturedly.

The reporters chuckled.

Another reporter asked, "Miss Moon, what do you have to say about your resemblance to film star, Jean Harlow?"

Mona answered, "If I looked half as beautiful as Jean Harlow, I would be thrilled."

"Is your white hair natural or dyed?"

Grinning, Mona answered, "Only my beautician knows for sure. Next question."

"Why are you here?"

"His Grace asked me to visit his beautiful estate, so I accepted. As simple as that."

"Is it true that you are the richest woman in the United States?"

Mona blushed. "No, that is not true. One more question."

A tall, thin man excitedly broke through the throng of reporters.

Startled, Mona looked to see if he had a gun in his hand.

"How long will you grace our country, Miss Moon?" the man asked, holding a camera.

"Not as long as I would wish. I would like to visit all of Great Britain, but I have duties at home in Kentucky."

Another reporter shouted, "Is it true that you are secretly a Bolshevik?"

The other reporters, irritated at first at the question, studied Mona's face, ready to write down her response.

"I assure you gentlemen, I am no Bolshevik," Mona denied. "I believe in free enterprise."

The tall, thin reporter continued his harassing of Mona. "You hire black men at the same wages as white men. You have instituted learning programs with your employees. Is it true that you are a radical? Do you want to overthrow the government of the United States? Who's responsible for the Depression?"

Robert frowned. "Thank you, gentlemen, but we have a train to catch." He escorted Mona and Violet away from the reporters.

"Won't you answer my questions, Miss

Moon?" the reporter called out to Mona. "Are you afraid to answer?"

Mona stopped and turned. "I won't because no matter what I say, you will twist my words. Good day to you gentlemen."

Robert, Mona, and Violet walked past the reporters toward their waiting cab.

A photographer snapped a picture of Violet.

As she turned to face the photographer, she recognized him as the man who almost pushed her overboard trying to get past her on the ship ramp. Realizing that his bump into her must have been premeditated, Violet hurried into the car with Mona and Robert, thinking this trip was full of potholes and blind spots. It was going to be a bumpy visit.

2

Mona and Violet checked into a two-bedroom suite at the Savoy. Two of her men checked into the suite opposite Mona's. The other two Pinkertons registered as American businessmen and took two separate rooms on the same floor. The last two Pinkertons shadowed Robert, who had a room on a separate floor. Appearances must be kept.

After instructing the hotel staff that she didn't want maid service, Mona felt more secure inside her suite. The reporter accusing her of being a Bolshevik shook Mona to her core. It was becoming more and more dangerous for her to express public opinions. Mrs. Eleanor Roosvelt, the First Lady, had warned Mona that she was no longer a private citizen and must be two steps ahead of those who wanted to use Mona for their own purposes. William Donovan, FDR's gentleman undercover agent, had said much the same thing when Mona had encountered German spies in Washington, D.C.

Mona and Violet quietly sat on the couch as one of the Pinkertons searched the suite for listening devices and anything that seemed out of place. The hotel had placed a large welcome fruit basket on the suite's coffee table which the Pinkerton man returned to hotel management. Mona didn't eat anything that came as so-called gifts.

It was a lifelong habit of not allowing anyone in her private rooms except for trusted people such as Violet. At Moon Manor in the Bluegrass, Mona always kept her bedroom suite locked and never allowed cleaning staff inside. This policy saved her the worry of staff snooping or someone poisoning her water carafe. If a hotel room needed cleaning, Violet and Mona stood watch until the maids retired. It was not a lifestyle that Mona enjoyed, but she found such safety precautions necessary ever since she had worked in Mesopotamia. She had hoped that since coming back to the States, such measures would prove to be unnecessary, but it was not to be so. Mona was on her guard more than ever.

Mona thanked the Pinkerton before he left to search his room and told Violet she was going to take a nap.

"Shall I get out an evening dress from the trunks and ready it for you, Miss Mona?"

"No, thank you, Violet. I think I shall be casual this evening."

"We're not eating in the dining room tonight?"

"I don't think so. I don't want to run into Herr Ribbentrop if he is really staying here."

"Oh," Violet said, disappointed that they were not eating at the Savoy. She had heard the food was outstanding.

"Violet, why don't you take a hot bath and a nap as well?"

Seeing that Violet looked disappointed and was itching to explore London, Mona capitulated. "All right. Go on, but be in your room an hour before dark. Take one of the Pinkertons with you, Violet, and I mean it."

"Yes, Miss Mona. I'll be back way before

dark. I promise."

Mona watched Violet giddily snatch her purse, hat, and gloves before rushing out of the suite. She stood in the doorway, making sure Violet enlisted a Pinkerton before leaving. Witnessing an excited Violet and a disheartened older Pinkerton catch the elevator, Mona chuckled and locked her suite door. After peeking at her Longines wrist watch, Mona wanted some downtime and gave the desk orders that she was not to receive phone calls or visitors. She wanted no one to bother her.

Not even Robert Farley.

3

Mona was awakened by insistent knocking on her bedroom door. She sat up and looked out the window. It was dusk.

"Miss Mona, are you awake?"

"Just a minute, Violet." Mona got out of bed, put on a robe, and unlocked her bedroom door.

Seeing Mona disheveled, Violet grimaced. "Did I wake you?"

"It's fine. I needed to get up anyway." Mona looked at Violet's animated expression. "Everything okay?"

Violet followed Mona into the living area of the suite. "I thought you should know something."

"What is that?"

"Herr Ribbentrop *is* staying at the Savoy. I

just saw him downstairs in the hotel's lobby talking to some of those Nazi fellows."

Mona pushed back her untidy hair. "How did you know they were Nazis?"

"They were wearing swastika armbands," Violet said, sitting beside Mona.

Mona raised an eyebrow. "I guess that is a good indication. How many were there?"

"Just two. Ribbentrop was making sure they were noticed, speaking real loud and gesturing."

"Did you catch their names or what they were saying?"

Violet said, "Ribbentrop caught sight of me as I was entering the hotel and tried to introduce me to them. I told him I was in a hurry and begged him to forgive my rudeness."

"It seems he keeps trying to insinuate himself into our circle."

"For what purpose?" Violet wondered.

"I would suspect there was a photographer close by. Ribbentrop would stop people of note coming through the lobby and invite them to meet his friends. The photographer would snap a picture of the group, making it seem like the unsuspecting person or persons were sympathetic to the Nazi cause. The Nazis would keep these photographs on file and use them for propaganda or blackmail later on as they saw fit—thus the arm bands with the swastikas."

"That's awful."

"It's politics, I'm afraid. We must do our best to stay out of European affairs and follow Robert's lead on this. After all, the prevailing sentiment in the United States is pro-isolationism at the moment."

"I'm so glad I ran past them."

"That was very wise of you, Violet."

"That's not all."

"What are you trying to say?"

"I went around the hall corner and hid, stopping to snoop, but Ribbentrop stayed out in the lobby with his friends for about ten more minutes."

"Violet, that is so dangerous with a man like him. He is a confidant of Adolph Hitler."

"How do you know that?"

"William Donovan gave me a list of known German agents before I left the States. Ribbentrop's name was on it."

"No wonder you wanted to be shed of him."

"I want to be cautious and not make mistakes, especially if my actions might embarrass Robert or Moon Enterprises."

"Don't you want to know what he did?"

Curious, Mona said, "I'll bite."

"He went into a small salon off the lobby where he met with a woman."

Mona was very interested now. "Describe her."

"She was a slight woman with dark hair parted in the middle. Very well dressed with expensive jewelry. Spoke with an upper class accent, but was American."

"An American?"

"Yes, and she acted American."

"How do we act differently from the British, Violet?" Mona was glad that Violet was picking up on cues.

"We walk differently and close the space between us and others when speaking. I've noticed the British are more reserved in their movement and speech."

Impressed with Violet's observations, Mona asked, "Did you hear what they were saying?"

"No, but the woman handed Ribbentrop a packet of letters."

"What kind of letters? In what type of envelopes?"

"They looked like letters on ivory linen stationery with some kind of important-looking crest on the top right. Looked official, but they were too far away for me to get a good look at the crest."

"What did Ribbentrop do with the letters?"

"He put them in his coat pocket. The two talked for a few minutes more and then she left."

"Were there others in the salon?"

"No, they were alone."

"Hotel staff?"

"No."

"Did Ribbentrop see you?"

"No, I scurried back here when the woman stood up."

"So you did not see the woman leave?"

Violet shook her head.

"She might still be in the hotel. Did the Pinkerton see her as well?"

"He went upstairs to his room."

Mona thought for a moment. "I will tell Robert what you saw, but you stay mum about it."

"Okay."

Mona paused, glancing at the window. "It's dark now. Violet, do you want to sample the London nightlife before we leave for Brynelleth?"

Violet brightened. "You bet I do."

"Then borrow one of my dresses and wear the hat with the veil."

"What for?"

"I want you to be my decoy. You're going to pose as me when you go out. Robert and I want one evening alone without reporters hounding our every move, and it will give the hotel maids one less thing to gossip about."

Violet understood Mona's meaning. "Sure, I can do that. It will be fun."

Mona smiled. "Thank you for understanding. Once we land on Brynelleth's doorstep, Robert and I won't have a moment to ourselves."

"May I wear some of your jewelry?"

"I have a nice pearl necklace that will suit you perfectly."

"I was hoping to wear the ruby tiara."

Mona laughed. "You're a cheeky one. The pearl necklace will do fine. Make sure you take two Pinkertons with you. They may act as your escorts."

"What if I meet a handsome, rich English aristocrat who wants to dance all night?"

"Just as long as the Pinkertons have their eyes on you. You better hurry and dress. I've ordered tickets to the new Noel Coward play in town."

"What is it?"

"*Conversation Piece.* It's a comedy musical."

"Oh, boy! I can't wait. I'm getting dressed right now." Violet rushed to her bedroom while Mona called the Pinkerton's suite. She needed to see all six of the bodyguards immediately, even the one guarding His Grace.

Mona dressed hurriedly in a pair of silk trousers and a cream-colored blouse. A few minutes later, she heard Violet let the Pinkertons in the suite. Mona came out and addressed them.

They tried to hide their embarrassment at seeing Mona wear pants. They had seen her wear them at Moon Manor, but London was a different matter. Still, she signed their checks, so they tried to act nonchalant.

Mona gave instructions that two Pinkertons were to accompany Violet to the play and dancing at the Savoy afterwards. The tickets were to be picked up at the box office, and money for the evening had been left at the front desk.

Two of the younger Pinkertons immediately volunteered. They were itching to do something fun before they headed to the dull countryside and the confined atmosphere of Brynelleth. Violet was a pretty girl, who laughed easily at their jokes, so they were most happy to escort Violet, especially since the tickets were for box seats. It would be an easy assignment.

"Do not detour," Mona admonished. "No jazz clubs. No pubs."

The youngest Pinkerton joked, "No opium dens."

His superior frowned at the young man for taking liberties with their boss.

Mona chuckled. "That's right. The play and then straight back to the Savoy. Remember Violet needs to be here by midnight. We are expected at Brynelleth for lunch. His Grace, Violet, and I will be taking the train, but three of you will be heading to His Grace's estate by car first thing in the morning. Our trunks will go with you."

"We'll make sure everything is shipshape before you arrive, Miss Mona," said Mr. Mott, the Pinkerton in charge.

"Make sure a car is sent for us at the train station," Mona advised.

"Yes, Miss," replied the head Pinkerton, nodding.

"Very good. You may go. Thank you." After the Pinkertons left, Mona spent the next hour helping to put the finishing touches on Violet which included the hat with the veil. "Now scoot and have a good time. Be back by the witching hour, young lady."

"I will. I promise," Violet said, rushing to open the suite's door when a knock sounded.

There stood the two young Pinkertons freshly scrubbed and shaven in their best suits. "Ready, Miss Violet?"

Violet glanced back at Mona. "I'll be back by midnight."

"Have a good time and don't take any wooden nickels."

As soon as Violet left, Mona locked the suite door and readied herself for the evening. Changing into a sheer pink negligee with ostrich feathers on the cuffs, Mona dabbed Vol de Nuit perfume on her throat and checked her makeup. Mona decided she looked as good as she was going to get and waited in the living area of the suite after opening the French doors leading to a balcony.

A special knock of three taps sounded on the door. Picking up her revolver, Mona answered the door.

"Put that thing away before you accidentally shoot me," Robert groused, entering the room with fish and chips takeaway rolled in newspaper.

"I see you ditched your bodyguard."

"I gave him the slip when you had a meeting with the Pinkertons, but I left him a message when I would be back so he wouldn't worry." He looked at Mona and whistled. "Them some rags you've got on, honey, and I like what's underneath, but I can do without the peashooter."

Mona put down the gun and sat beside Robert on the couch. "Oh, it's so good to be free of everyone and have some down time to be ourselves for a few hours."

"I'll say." Robert dropped the fish and chips on the coffee table and enfolded Mona in his arms, kissing her passionately. After they came up for air, Robert said, "How are we going to pull this off? I can hardly stand to be away from you, and now we have to act like vestal virgins."

Smiling, Mona said, "We have a few hours to be together before we face Brynelleth."

"Worried, darling?"

"Frankly, I am. I want to make a good impression, Robert. I want your people to accept me."

Robert pulled Mona close, setting his chin on her head. "You will, Mona, and I'll be with you every step of the way." He kissed her hair as they sat quietly for a few moments with Mona leaning into Robert.

Feeling his stomach rumbling, Robert asked, "Hungry? Let's eat up. Last time for fish and chips before those dreary overcooked beef dinners with tomato aspic at Brynelleth."

"Did you get ketchup?"

"We use vinegar in Merry Old England. If you ask for ketchup, the help will think you are a barbarian."

Amused, Mona opened the newspaper and then a paper lining revealing hot battered fish with potato wedges. She picked apart a fillet and ate it with her fingers. "Um, divine. So tender."

Robert did the same. "The only thing missing

is mushy peas."

Mona shuddered. Robert had cooked mushy peas before, but they were not to her liking. "If you say so."

Good-naturedly, Robert cuffed Mona's chin.

"Hey, now. You're hitting the future Duchess of Brynelleth."

"I'd rather do this." Robert lifted Mona's chin and gave her a sloppy kiss. "Hmm, vinegar and salt."

"You'd better eat something before I start in on your fish and chips," Mona said, laughing.

Robert unfolded the newspaper for his fish and chips order, letting the steam roll out. He ate with gusto.

Both Mona and Robert said little while eating their takeaway and gazing at the bright lights of London shining through the French doors. They could hear the bustling traffic below in the streets, which were filled with throngs of busy people and honking taxis.

Listening to the commotion, Mona paused eating. She and Robert had a difficult few months ahead of them at Brynelleth, and Mona was worried if she was up to the task of becoming mistress of such a large estate plus handling her own business affairs.

Seeing concern splashed on Mona's face, Robert rose and closed the French doors. "Let's shut out the world for the next couple of hours, Mona. Shall we? We'll worry about Brynelleth tomorrow."

Mona nodded enthusiastically.

Robert picked Mona up and carried her into the bedroom, kicking the door shut with his foot. The next few hours were for the two of them. The rest of the world be damned.

4

The next morning, Mona, Robert, Violet, and three Pinkertons took the train from London to the village nearest Robert's home. Instead of the expected estate cars and drivers, Mr. Mott and one other Pinkerton waited for them in rented utilitarian vehicles. Mona, Robert, and Violet took one car with Mr. Mott driving, while the four remaining Pinkertons piled in the last car.

Twenty minutes later, the cars passed through formidable iron gates, past a stone gatehouse, and proceeded up a winding drive. The months of anticipation about this moment took hold of Mona and she reached over to clasp Robert's hand, intertwining her fingers with his.

He responded with a comforting smile, but his eyes seemed fretful.

As the car rounded the final bend, Mona got her first glimpse of Brynelleth through the trees. She stopped herself before gasping out loud as the manor stood seemingly ancient and monstrous, sprawled out against a cloudy sky threatening to rain. Four imposing turrets dominated the three story structure. Its gloomy walls were covered with ivy, and moss was growing on the foundation stones. Its many windows were hidden behind thorny bushes. Clunky annexes of later architectural styles had been added on the opposite sides of the main medieval structure. Behind the manor rose a looming stone tower dominating the main structure. There were no graceful columns or inviting porticos. The facade seemed jumbled and there was no symmetry or harmony to the structure at all.

The driveway was mainly dirt sprouting weeds as the pea gravel had mostly disappeared. The fountain in front of the manor was spewing a small stream of green scum. Mona couldn't even figure out where the main door was as there were several entrances. She couldn't help but feel concern that she had agreed to pour money into this crumbling structure. The Farley ancestral manor seemed menacing if not ominously hostile to Mona. She shuddered thinking she might have to call this relic her home.

Violet was correct. Brynelleth was glorious all right—gloriously hideous.

Sensing Mona's discomfort as they came into full view of the house, Robert held her kid-gloved hand even more tightly. He explained quickly, "Brynelleth was built in the 1500s during the Tudor reign. Since then, each Farley has tried to put his own stamp on Brynelleth, thus the different building styles. As you can see it has resulted in a mishmash of architectural whims."

"Your family goes back that far?" Mona asked, incredulously. Mona could tell Robert was embarrassed, almost bashful, about the condition of his estate.

"I told you my family was once royalty. To-day, we're just nobility."

"Brynelleth goes back further than the 1500s, Robert. That tower looks medieval."

"It began life as a fortress built by William the Conquer. A Norman family had it for centuries and they died out. Brynelleth was abandoned for several hundred years and then Henry Tudor VII bequeathed it with a land grant to my ancestor."

"Henry VIII's father, huh? Do you know the reason for the bequeathal?"

"To repay a debt that King Henry VII owed my ancestor. Other than that, I don't know much. I've never bothered to do the research."

The car stopped in front of the main entrance, or at least, Mona assumed it was the main entrance. It was hard to tell from the jumble of doors on the front of the manor through the now down-pouring rain. It was raining so hard that the water droplets were falling sideways due to the howling wind.

The Pinkerton at the wheel of the hired car honked his horn prompting a man dressed in a butler's attire and white gloves to rush out from a battered wooden door with an umbrella in hand. Mr. Mott followed with an umbrella also.

Helping Mona emerge from the car, Robert growled, "Why weren't we met with the Bentley at the train station, Finch?"

"I'm sorry, Your Grace, but the car needs repairs. That's why the Pinkerton chaps hired rentals for you."

"What about the work vehicles?"

"I'm afraid they are on the mend as well."

"All our cars need repairs?"

"I'm afraid so, Your Grace."

Mona interrupted, "Robert, can this wait? I'm getting soaked."

"So sorry, dear." Robert took off his coat and held it over Mona's head as they rushed from the car into the foyer and then the great hall.

Violet and the three Pinkertons riding in another car scampered inside behind them.

Mona laughed at the absurdity of their introduction to Brynelleth, thinking she must look like a drowned rat. Handing Robert back his coat and trying to smooth her hair after taking off her Robin Hood hat with its sodden droopy feathers, Mona looked up to see the entire staff of Brynelleth staring at her. Men stood on one side and women on the other. In the middle stood a middle-aged matron with a solemn expression on her inquisitive face.

"Oh, good Lord," Mona whispered, thinking she must be a sight.

"Steady on, girl," Robert whispered out of the side of his mouth. "This is your first test." He handed his coat to Finch and putting his arm around Mona, he announced, "I would like to introduce my fiancée, Miss Mona Moon. I know you will serve her as you did my mother, the late Duchess of Brynelleth."

Mona pulled away from Robert, saying, "Good morning to you all. I hope to prove to be as good a mistress as Robert's mother. I assure you I will do my best to honor this house."

The housekeeper stepped forward. "We welcome our master home again. His Grace has been gone far too long."

Mona recognized the subtle jab at Robert, but chose to ignore it. As with all servants who proved to be difficult, Mona chose to take command. Looking quite imperial, Mona said, "Please introduce yourself."

"Forgive me, Miss. My name is Mrs. Birdwhistle. I am the housekeeper." She nodded to one of the maids who stepped forward, curtsied, and presented Mona with a bouquet of flowers. "These are from our gardens, Miss."

"Thank you." Mona inhaled the scent of the flowers. "This most pleases me. I have extensive gardens at Moon Manor, so I'm pleased to find the same at Brynelleth."

"Our garden was designed by Capability Brown in 1769."

"I look forward to visiting it."

"May I present the staff?" Mrs. Birdwhistle said, trying not to stare at Mona's platinum hair.

Mona knew the rest of the staff was sneaking peeks at her as well. She must be a strange spectacle with her wet white hair and queer yellow eyes. This was not the dignified introduction she had hoped for with Robert's household staff.

Mrs. Birdwhistle waved a hand to a thin, nervous woman dressed in a long dark dress and white cap with wisps of gray hair escaping. "This is Cook, Mrs. Wicket."

Mrs. Wicket wiped her damp hands on her stark white apron before curtsying and giving Mona a quick smile. There was much vitality and joie de vivre in her manner.

"Nice to meet you, Mrs. Wicket. I'm sure you will put on a fine table for us."

Blushing, Mrs. Wicket answered, "I'll do my best to make you proud, Miss Moon."

Mona nodded, knowing she had made an ally

in the house.

Mrs. Birdwhistle moved to the next woman in line. "This is Mrs. Rymer, who will act as your personal secretary."

Mrs. Rymer, dressed in her best navy Sunday dress and new silk stockings, curtsied. Speaking very fast with the words tumbling right up against each other, she said, "I served as the Duchess' social secretary for many years before she passed away." She looked at Robert for confirmation.

"Then I'm sure you will act with the same discretion for me as you did for the last Duchess of Brynelleth," Mona said.

Mrs. Rymer nodded, noting the unspoken message in Mona's words—*don't take my business into the street or you'll be fired.*

Mona greeted the remaining staff—parlor maids, house maids, chamber maids, scullery maids, kitchen maids, laundry maids, tea boy, first footman, second footman, and undercook—for the next five minutes before she introduced Violet as her companion.

The staff stared at Violet as though she was an enigma. She seemed to them a fresh faced, smiling American dressed in the latest fashion—a chiffon periwinkle flower pattern dress with a ruffle collar plus a dark blue jacket with matching blue shoes and purse—and, of course, white gloves. To top it off, Violet wore a pearl necklace. In England, this expensive outfit was worn only by the upper class, who could afford the complete ensemble—not poorly paid ladies' companions who had to resort to wearing repaired stockings, mismatched handbags and shoes with their dresses. In other words, Violet dressed *above her station*. A lady of means never functioned as a great lady's companion, so who was this girl? The staff immediately disliked her.

Violet stepped forward and declared, "Hello. It's nice to meet y'all."

Robert tried not to smile at Violet's decidedly Southern drawl, which he found enchanting. Noticing the staff's pinched stares at Violet, he said, "I'm sure you will make all my guests feel welcome and serve them to your utmost ability."

The staff murmured, "Yes, Your Grace."

Robert rubbed his hands together in anticipation. "Now that introductions have been settled, we are famished, Finch."

"Yes, My Lord, I mean Your Grace."

"I know, Finch. The new title takes some getting used to."

"Thank you, Your Grace." Finch spoke to Mona. "We hope lunch meets with your approval, Miss."

"I'm sure any time you and Mrs. Birdwhistle prepare a meal we'll be eatin' high off the hog as we say down home."

Finch gave Mona an odd look.

Robert lowered his head, but couldn't contain his amusement. He laughed, saying, "Finch, get used to it. Americans like to walk the long way around a barn when they are not being blunt."

Finch was ill at ease with the American, but wanted the staff to make a good impression with their future mistress. "I see what you are saying, Your Grace." He looked at Mona. "You like to speak in idioms, Miss Moon?"

"I like to speak so that my meaning gets across. Get my drift?"

Finch cleared his throat. "Indeed, I do, Miss Moon. Wilbert will show you to the dining room."

Robert held up his hand. "I know the way, Finch."

Nodding, Finch said, "Of course, Your Grace."

Robert walked Mona through the great hall, which was lined with portraits of ancestors, suits of armor, various medieval weapons hanging on the panelled walls, and over the massive fireplace. "This is where we have our fetes."

Mona glanced up at the two-story ceiling with stained glass windows reaching most of the way up. "How do you heat this place?"

"We don't. The English are used to homes without central heat. We prefer fireplaces."

"Fireplaces don't provide much warmth."

"No, they don't. Just bundle up," Robert answered as he guided Mona and Violet down a hallway and to the right with Mrs. Rymer following. "Here we go." He led them into a large room with a mammoth dining table topped with silver candelabras holding beeswax candles. Mona counted twenty-six chairs. A fresh flower arrangement adorned the middle of the table, which gleamed from polishing as did the silver candelabras. The sideboards hosted bottles of wine and cordials while place settings of exquisite hand painted, flower patterned china sat at either end of the table with two settings placed in the middle. Mona could tell much care was taken in presenting a beautiful display.

She quickly glanced at the markings on the back of a plate. "Robert, do you know this bone china is from Josiah Spode's factory?"

"Mother did put much store by this particular set. I'm afraid I don't know much about porcelain. Why so interested?"

"It's bone china, not porcelain. Let's just say this bone china belongs in a museum. Here, hold a plate up to the light. You can see the outline of your hand through it."

"Good, maybe we can sell it and pay for the roof."

Mona grinned. "Over my dead body." She looked at the place settings and instantly decided there was no way she was going to be seated at the end of the table at least twenty feet away from Robert.

"Finch."

"Yes, Miss Moon."

"Tell your staff that they have set a handsome table, but His Grace and I have much business to discuss over lunch, so we need to sit closer.

Would you please put my place setting next to the Duke's?"

"Discussing business over lunch?" Finch wondered out loud. He waved to the table. "This is how the late Duke and Duchess preferred to have their seating arranged at the table."

Patting Finch's shoulder, Robert said, "It's alright, Finch. Father and Mother won't mind. Just give my lady what she wants. We don't want to spend our first luncheon at Brynelleth shouting at each other."

"If you insist, Your Grace."

"I do, and let's be quick about it. I want to show Miss Moon Brynelleth Manor this afternoon."

"Very good, Your Grace." Finch ordered Wilbert, the First Footman, and Keelan, the Second Footman, to move Mona's china, silverware, and crystal glasses to the immediate left of Robert's chair. Mona was seated by Wilbert, the First Footman, and then the two footmen pulled the chairs out for Violet and Mrs. Rymer.

Robert seated himself and snapped open his napkin. "I'm famished. We had a very skimpy breakfast this morning."

Wilbert and Keelan served a lunch of sliced tender roast beef topped by a hearty gravy and buttered whole potatoes, carrots, and peas accompanied by cottage loaf bread. A cinnamon custard followed as the dessert.

Mona tried not to show her impatience with Finch and the two footmen hovering and standing behind their chairs waiting to serve. It was hard to hold a conversation with Robert when servants were listening to everything the two said during lunch.

Noticing Mona's discomfort, Robert leaned over and mumbled, "Just pretend they are not there."

That was hard to do. At Moon Manor, the staff ventured into the kitchen after serving and only appeared again if Mona rang a bell. A footman standing behind her chair was something that she was going to have to get used to. Finished, Mona put the knife and fork parallel on her plate. "Finch, please tell Mrs. Wicket lunch was delicious. The peas were so fresh, and I've never had so wonderful a custard."

"Cook will be grateful to hear," Finch replied.

Robert stood and threw down his napkin.

"Yes, it was a perfect lunch. Tell Cook we approve."

Finch nodded, undoubtedly pleased with Robert's response. Wilbert rushed to help Mona out of her chair.

She murmured, "Thank you."

Robert grabbed Mona's hand pulling her away from the footman's ministrations. They stepped out into the hallway near the grand staircase. "Ready for a tour, darling?"

"I think I would like a bit of a rest first. It's been a long day already. May Violet and I be taken to our rooms?"

"Of course." Robert looked at his watch. "I shall come for you about three o'clock then?"

Mona nodded and pressed a quick kiss on Robert's cheek. "Don't bother showing me to my room, Robert. Mrs. Birdwhistle can do that." Mona turned as the housekeeper stepped out of the shadows of the stairwell. "Mrs. Birdwhistle, I'm going to have to put a bell around your neck so I know when you are about."

"Where in the blazes did you come from, Mrs. Birdwhistle?" Robert snapped. He had always disliked the habit of Brynelleth's servants sneaking up on him, but he could hardly blame them as they were taught not to be noticed or heard by the gentry. It was so different in Moon Manor. One could always hear the staff whistling, laughing, joking, vacuuming, chitchatting, banging pots in the kitchen, or Chloe barking about the house. The silence at Brynelleth was, strange to say—deafening.

"I'm sorry, Your Grace. I'm ready to show you to your suite, if you care to follow me, Miss Moon."

Mona made a face at Robert behind Mrs. Birdwhistle's back, which caused Robert to chuckle. "Mrs. Birdwhistle, did you receive the instructions I wired?" Mona said, climbing the stairs behind Mrs. Birdwhistle.

"Yes, Miss." Reaching the landing, Mrs. Birdwhistle turned left and went down a hallway that led to the back of the house. She stopped at the last door. "His Grace instructed that you were to have his mother's bedroom. It oversees the lake and the garden."

"Oh, I didn't realize," Mona said, looking back at Violet, who was several steps behind her.

"It is the only suite in the manor that has its

own bathroom. Other bedrooms have to share."

"I wanted a suite in which Miss Violet could sleep as well."

"There is a nurse's bedroom that is connected. I think it will be suitable." Mrs. Birdwhistle opened the door and beckoned the two women inside.

Mona and Violet stepped into a large room of which two sides were floor to ceiling windows with flowing white gauzy curtains.

Mrs. Birdwhistle walked over to one of the windows and opened it. "You have a view of the gardens, the lake, and if you look beyond the tree line, you can see a sliver of the sea."

Mona and Violet peered out the window.

"I think this is the loveliest room in the house," Mrs. Birdwhistle said, proudly.

"The view is astounding," Mona concurred. She gazed about the room with its vases filled with garden flowers gracing polished furniture, new bedclothes, and scrubbed floors. In the corners stood large, colorful ceramic containers boasting large house plants from the greenhouse. The walls were covered with white wallpaper with hand stamped pale images of ferns and yellow birds. The muted colors of the wallpaper went well with the pale green silk coverlet and white crisp sheets embellishing the four poster bed. The furniture was painted white, which was a delightful change from the heavy dark furniture elsewhere in Brynelleth. Faded Persian rugs adorned the wooden floors marked by years of wear. Somehow everything came together to give the bedroom an atmosphere of a calm and restful oasis.

Mona realized the staff had spent days getting this room ready for her occupancy and that the new pillows, sheets, blankets, and bedspread for her bed were costly. She wondered about the impact of these purchases on the household budget. She smiled back at a beaming Mrs. Birdwhistle and decided to delve into the matter later. "Please tell the staff that I appreciate their thoughtfulness."

"Yes, Miss."

Violet explored the bathroom, which she and Mona would share. Again the bathroom was sparkling though outdated with tiles missing from the walls.

Mrs. Birdwhistle walked over to a door. "This

is your room, Miss."

Violet peeked into a much smaller room with mahogany panelling and masculine dark furniture. Again, the bedclothes were new and flowers were placed on her nightstand.

"I hope you both will be comfortable."

Mona said, "Thank you, Mrs. Birdwhistle."

"Shall I unpack for you, Miss?" asked Mrs. Birdwhistle, looking at the steamer trunks sitting in the middle of the room.

"I shall see to it myself. You may go now."

Mrs. Birdwhistle looked a bit hurt, but pointed to an embroidered strap dangling from the ceiling near the bed. "If you should need anything, ring the bell."

Mona nodded and waited for Mrs. Birdwhistle to leave.

Mrs. Birdwhistle reluctantly left the bedroom, knowing the downstairs staff would be disappointed not knowing what Mona Moon had brought in her trunks. The women were especially interested in Mona's cosmetics, jewelry, evening gowns, and underclothes.

As soon as the housekeeper left, Violet locked the door with the skeleton key left in the lock.

"You didn't ask for her key to the room."

"It doesn't matter. I'm having the locks changed this afternoon." Mona looked about the bedroom. "I feel honored to be put up in the late Duchess' room. I know the servants worked hard on getting it ready. Robert told me the room had not been used in years."

"Did you notice the napkins at lunch?"

"Yes, the lace edging was tattered."

Violet offered, "The napkin material is good linen though. If I had help, I could repair the lace and the napkins would be good as new."

"I think tomorrow we should do an inventory of all the linens in the manor and determine what needs to be repaired and what we need to purchase."

"I'll see if they have a sewing machine," Violet said.

"Well, let's unpack." Mona looked at her watch. "We just have enough time before the Pinkertons arrive with their report."

Violet dragged her trunk into her room and gently hung her dresses in a small wardrobe, placed her gloves and underthings in the chest of drawers, stacked her shoes neatly under the bed, and stored her powder and perfume on the vanity possessing a large round mirror. As soon as she was finished, Violet went into the main bedroom and rearranged everything Mona had put away, fussing that her mistress did not know how to store clothing properly.

Mona didn't hear Violet's complaining as she was in a deep conversation with the head Pinkerton, Mr. Mott, who had arrived to give his report.

She didn't like what she was hearing.

5

"No one responsible for locking the doors and windows at night."

Mona said, "I thought the butler was accountable for locking up."

"Finch is forgetful. I think you might request that he retire and let the first footman take over," Mr. Mott reported, having arrived the night before with two of the Pinkertons and discovered the manor in chaos.

Mona pressed her lips together. "I think that would cause a small rebellion if I start making employee changes. I need these people to trust me."

The Pinkerton insisted, "Anybody could break in. A child could do it. I've never seen so lax a security protocol."

"England is considered a law and order country."

"So is the United States, but that didn't stop someone from breaking into the Lindbergh home and abducting their baby."

"I know. I know. The world is changing," Mona replied, sadly.

"Look—most of the locks in this place are over a hundred years old. They don't work or if they do, the keys are missing, so most of the locks need to be replaced."

"Is there thieving going on?"

"The maids tell me there is, but that's not the point. It's only a matter of time before a person is hired who steals you blind instead of committing petty thievery, especially when it comes to petrol, the house silver, and the kitchen larder. Even here, times are hard."

Frustrated that security was essentially non-existent, Mona inquired, "Did you ask for a household inventory list?"

"Yes, Miss Mona. The last one was done forty years ago."

"So long ago?"

"I've been told by Finch that after the late

Duchess passed away, the Duke just let things go to pot."

"You mean Robert's father?"

"Yes, Miss." The Pinkerton realized that Mona was becoming increasingly irritated, but he hadn't delivered the worst news yet.

"May I have the list please?"

The Pinkerton unzipped his case and handed Mona a folder.

"Oh, good Lord," Mona moaned, opening the folder and glancing at the list. "It's not typed, but written in long hand and in pencil. It's so faded, I can barely read it." She handed the list to Violet, who sat next to her on the couch in the sitting area by the window.

"I can make out some of the entries," Violet replied. "It looks much like my great aunt's writing. I could always make out the chicken scratch on her grocery list."

Mona leaned toward the Pinkerton. "Let's start with this. Hire a photographer to photograph all the rooms in the manor including the contents in the closets. That will give us a frame of reference, and we can compare the old inventory list with the photographs. We'll start with the main rooms, the bedrooms, the attic, and the servants' wings. We've got to get a handle on what is here."

"That is not in my job description to hire help, Miss. It's not what I do."

"I'm aware of that, but everyone is going to have to pitch in if we want to go home on schedule."

"All right, Miss, but you need to hire a secretary to help with such matters."

Ignoring the Pinkerton's complaint, Mona said, "Get Mrs. Birdwhistle to suggest a photographer. Now for the security issues, is there someone in the manor who is fond of dogs? I haven't seen one canine on this estate."

"I understand that they had a kennel at one time, but it is no longer maintained."

"That doesn't answer my question."

"The tea boy, Todd, seems to have a fondness for animals."

"Yes, I noticed him. How old is he?"

"He's sixteen."

"I see. He will be in charge of the dogs. Buy two male puppies who will be the house guard dogs and have them trained." Mona thought of

Chloe and missed her terribly, but knew the poodle was better left at Moon Manor.

"I'll see if I can find two German Shepherds."

Mona laughed. "I think *German* Shepherds would cause a fuss, even though they are fine guard dogs. See if you can find two English Mastiffs."

"Mastiffs are clumsy and none too bright."

Mona waved the Pinkerton's concerns away. "But they are English bred dogs and loyal to a fault. They will notify the staff if someone comes to the house, and the mere sight of them is intimidating."

Trying to hide his irritation, the Pinkerton said, "Yes, Miss Mona." He couldn't risk making Mona angry. After all, Mona gave out Christmas bonuses to all her employees, and he didn't want to jeopardize his. If Mona Moon wanted English Mastiffs, he would find them for her. If she wanted him to hire a photographer, he would do it. He couldn't afford to lose his job as he had a family to support—and he wanted to get back to the States as soon as possible for he was homesick.

"When is the locksmith coming?"

"He's already here, Miss, changing the locks on the downstairs entrance doors."

"Make sure you get a list of the keys for every lock he changes and see that I get a copy. He is not to keep any masters. I want everything."

"Yes, Miss."

"Have Mrs. Rymer type up the key list if she is still here."

"Yes, Miss."

"Is there anything else to report?"

The Pinkerton hesitated for a moment before soldiering on. Drawing in a large breath, he quickly said, "It's about the ghosts, Miss."

Mona gave him a sharp glance. "What ghosts?"

"Brynelleth has a history of being haunted."

"All these old houses have stories about ghosts. Goes with the territory."

"The servants complained of haunting recently—strange noises like footsteps and scratching, missing items, and unexplained lights. Even one of my men reported seeing an apparition last night, Miss. I wouldn't take this lightly."

Alarmed, Violet asked, "What kind of apparition?"

"During his rounds, one of my men saw a woman in a white dress descending the main staircase. When he called out to her, she vanished."

"Why are female ghosts always floating about in white dresses?" Mona asked.

"You said several ghosts?" Violet asked, wide-eyed.

"My men also reported strange flickering lights in the oldest part of the manor. When they check the Norman castle annex, they feel like they are being watched and the atmosphere seems charged."

"All this in one night? I'm sure there is an explanation for these events. Once all the locks are changed and dogs are living in the manor, I think you will see a cessation of these incidents. This goes to show that security needs to improve drastically. We are having a problem with flesh and blood trespassers—not spirits."

Unconvinced, the head Pinkerton said, "If you say so, Miss."

Mona stood. "I think that's all for today. Please send the locksmith up to me. I want to have the locks changed to this room before His

Grace comes for me at three o'clock."

The Pinkerton rose from his chair as well. "Thank you, Miss."

"Thank you. I appreciate your hard work."

"Yes, Miss Moon." Mr. Mott left the bedroom suite wondering where the locksmith was. It was hard keeping track of everyone in the manor. The building's complexity was significant, and there were so many employees about. Not like Moon Manor, which had a house staff of only ten persons.

As soon as he closed the door, Violet asked, "Do you think there are really ghosts here? I won't be able to sleep a wink tonight."

"I think the only ghosts at Brynelleth are servants playing tricks on the Americans. 'Let's give the Yanks a good scare'—that type of thing. Harmless enough. I wouldn't give those stories a second thought."

"But the lady disappeared on the staircase."

"Perhaps the electric lights weren't on, and the Pinkerton thought he saw something in the moonlight streaming through the great hall window. Moonlight can be deceiving, and the atmosphere at Brynelleth can be rather imposing."

"I think the place is creepy. Everything is run down. Have you noticed how cold it is here?"

"Brynelleth will take some getting used to, but put this ghost business behind you. It's nothing more than practical jokes played by the locals."

Violet seemed comforted at Mona's words, but what she didn't know was that Mona received a letter slipped under their suite door at the Savoy before they left for the train station. The message was comprised of magazine letters cut out and pasted on a piece of paper.

Stay away or the ghosts of Brynelleth will have their revenge!

Brynelleth gave Mona pause, filling her with foreboding. She couldn't wait to return to Moon Manor.

6

"Well, what do you think?" Robert asked, after giving Mona an extensive tour of the Brynelleth.

"I think Dexter Deatherage was right. Brynelleth needs a new roof."

"I thought you had hired workmen to repair it." Robert pulled out his cigarette case for a smoke.

Mona grabbed the cigarette and put it in her pocket. "Apparently they went on strike."

Annoyed, Robert asked, "Can you fix it with the workmen?"

Ignoring Robert's displeasure over his snatched cigarette, Mona leaned her head against Robert's shoulder. "I'll start on it early in the morning."

Robert gently patted Mona's cheek. He looked about the grand portrait hallway in which they were standing. "This place is appalling, isn't it?"

"Brynelleth does seem to lean on the ghastly side." Mona and Robert glanced at each other and broke into laughter.

"Oh, bloody hell, we should sell up and get out."

"And put all those who depend on Brynelleth for a living out of a job during a Depression! No, sir, Robert. We stick it out and try to make this place work."

"Mona, who are we kidding? It will take piles of money to make Brynelleth livable again."

"I have piles of money."

Robert hugged Mona, saying, "That's why I'm going to marry you—my rich American cow."

Mona playfully elbowed Robert, saying, "You know how I feel about you referring to me as a bovine."

Robert turned serious. "Really, darling, I have only eighty thousand pounds in a trust fund my grandmother left me. I can't touch the principal."

"This is the first I've heard of it. You've been holding out on me."

"I know that sounds like a lot of money, but it is needed to pay for our personal expenses during our lifetime and our children's education. It's what I used for collateral for the bank loans. All the money Brynelleth makes goes back into the property, and it's only enough to cover costs. Even then we are losing money."

"I thought you bought new farm equipment the last time you were here. Wasn't that investment to increase the yields of grain, hay, and vegetables?"

"The lads won't use them. They say the tractors are noisy and smell of gasoline. They prefer their draft horses."

"We are asking farmers to give up practices they have used for hundreds of years. My mother told me there was great resistance from people changing from horse-drawn carriages to gas-driven vehicles. It takes time for people to adjust to new technology."

"How do I drag these stubborn men into the twentieth century?" Robert asked, running his hand through his hair.

"Do you have any women farmers?"

"Several who work their own land."

"Commandeer the tiniest of the women and teach her how to drive the tractor. Give her a deal on its use. You charge for the use of the tractors, right?"

"Just for the gas and it's on the honor system. They are to put a coin or two in the rental box when the tractors are checked out."

Mona nodded. "Let's throw a barbeque for your farmers and demonstrate the new equipment. Have this woman plow with a tractor. Your young lads will come around after seeing a little woman drive a tractor. If your older farmers still want to use their draft horses, let them. Everything will work out in the end."

"What about the manor?"

"You're not going to like what I am to propose, but we are going to open Brynelleth to the public. It's the only way to save it."

"I had hoped it was not coming to that. We will be disgraced, of course. Considered upstarts."

"Or we will be considered innovators. We can't be the only estates hurting for money."

Seeing the worry lines of on Robert's forehead, Mona said, "I will do it bit by bit. I won't hit the staff with everything at once."

"When I was a boy, this house was filled with laughter. We had a staff of thirty people and a stable of fine horses. Our jumpers won competition ribbons and were sought after. We raised some of the finest cattle in England. My family was respected and admired. Our parties were famous and everyone desired an invitation. Then the war came. My brother was killed and Mother died of a broken heart. My father was left a bitter shell of a man, and I turned to drink to drown out the pain. I was of no use to him. Brynelleth fell into ruins."

"It's not too late to pick up the pieces. A lot is riding on how we handle this." When Robert didn't respond, Mona nudged him. "It will be fine, Robert. It's a new beginning for us all."

Robert closed his eyes, inhaled deeply, held his breath, and then exhaled sharply as if purging himself of the past. Opening his eyes, Robert said, "Yes, we should move forward. All is not lost."

"Shall we inform the staff of our intentions after tea?"

Robert teased, "Might as well. Let's just hope they don't poison us at dinner."

"Don't be such a worrywart. They'll see it is to their benefit."

"I have found that people resist change, even if it is a positive thing for them." Looking at his wristwatch, Robert announced, "It's tea time, darling. We need to adjourn to the library."

Mona hooked her arm around Robert's and realized she was hungry. A slice of yellow pound cake and a cup of hot tea were just what was needed before her talk with the staff.

7

Alarmed, Finch said, "I don't understand, Miss."

"It's simple. His Grace and I are splitting duties. He will concentrate on the estate, and I will handle Brynelleth Manor. I am making a sizeable financial commitment to this property as a wedding gift to His Grace, and we need to double our efforts to get it back into shape."

"But we are already understaffed, Miss Moon," Mrs. Birdwhistle complained. "What you are proposing is beyond our present capabilities."

Undeterred, Mona ordered, "First, we start with the mending and cleaning. Then we concentrate on repairs and upgrades."

Bewildered, Mrs. Birdwhistle said, "We've been cleaning for weeks, Miss Moon. I'm sorry that we have not lived up to your expectations."

"But you have, Mrs. Birdwhistle. I am ever so pleased, but more needs to be done—and fast."

"'Tis true," Mrs. Wicket said. "The kitchen could do with a good scrub down and a coat of paint."

Mrs. Birdwhistle shot Mrs. Wicket a nasty look.

"That's the way, Mrs. Wicket. Here's a list of things I want done in the next week." Mona handed Mrs. Birdwhistle a list. "Hire five women and several men from the village. I'll pay a pound at the end of each week, plus a bonus if they do an exceptional job."

"A pound for each week!" exclaimed one of the footmen.

Finch scowled at the footman's outburst.

"They'll earn it, believe me. Brynelleth staff will also see a bonus at the end of the month. Each person will be paid according to their contribution."

The staff murmured excitedly amongst themselves.

Finch ordered them to be quiet.

Pointing to Violet, Mona continued, "Miss

Violet will be in charge of the linen and bed-clothes. We will need two seamstresses. Anyone handy with a needle?"

"We have several local women who are known for their way around a spool of thread," one of the maids replied.

"That's good," Violet said. "One thing I've noticed is that everyone's uniform is in need of repair, so I would like everyone to have two new uniforms. I will need help with that. Also, I am a very good seamstress myself. If the ladies would like to have a new dress for their own use, give me the pattern with the material cut out, and I will sew it for you. Is the sewing machine down-stairs in good order? I noticed it this afternoon. It's a foot pedal machine with which I am acquainted, so that won't be any problem for me, but any electric sewing machines nearby?"

The laundry maid answered, "Yes, Miss Violet, and I have a friend who has another sewing machine we can use." The maid found it strange that Violet was referred to as Miss Violet rather than Miss Tate. Must be an American custom. Companions and maids of ladies were always referred by their last name.

"That's good, because we're going to need it," Violet said. "Miss Moon has opened an account at the local shop. For the next week, you can purchase patterns, cloth, buttons, thread, zippers, lace, soap, candy, personal hygiene articles, and hairbrushes. Each person has a limit of 1 pound sixpence."

"What about the men?" asked Finch.

"The same goes for them as well. I can also sew shirts, coats, trousers. All I need is a pattern and the cloth cut out ready to go."

The servants looked at Violet with renewed admiration. They had thought she was a puffball, but it looked like the young American was going to pull up her shirtsleeves and work alongside them. They were impressed.

"I can contact local women for the sewing and cleaning," offered Mrs. Rymer. "They would welcome the extra income."

"Make sure they understand they will have to work hard," Mona advised. "The first time I catch someone not pulling their weight, they're gone."

Mrs. Rymer, seemingly enthused at the prospect of returning Brynelleth to its former glory, said, "We shan't let Brynelleth down."

"Good. The seamstresses should report to Miss Violet, who will report to me. The extra cleaners will report to Mrs. Birdwhistle, who will report to me." Mona turned to the butler. "Finch, you are to work with the Pinkertons on security. Have the two footmen and Todd included in their briefings as well."

"Who's gonna cook for these people while they're here?" the undercook clucked. "I've got my hands full cooking for us now." This woman was responsible for cooking for the staff while Mrs. Wicket cooked for the family.

"What's your name?" Mona asked sternly.

Looking about for support from the staff, the woman answered, "Bertha, Miss."

"We will provide lunch at eleven and tea before they leave for the day at four. You know the farmers' wives. You know who are good cooks. Hire three of them to make stews and breads, plus tea cakes and glazed buns. I'll pay for the ingredients plus their work. I'll make it worth their while. You concentrate on reorganizing your station and cooking breakfast, as Mrs. Wicket will need your help with the kitchen clean up. I want those pots and pans to sparkle."

The undercook looked placated. "Thank you, Miss. I didn't mean to speak out of turn." She looked sheepishly at Mrs. Birdwhistle, who took no notice as she was busy reading the list Mona had handed her.

"I understand that what His Grace and I are asking is far and above your normal duties, but it will be worth it. We want to make Brynelleth a vital engine for the local economy again. That reminds me—Finch, I don't see the Farley coat of arms flying on top of the castle. Everyone should know His Grace has returned."

"I'll see to it, Miss."

"Very good. Any questions?" Mona waited for someone to speak up. "No? Then you are dismissed."

"Miss Moon, may I speak with you privately?" Mrs. Birdwhistle asked as the others returned to their duties.

"Come with me." Mona went into the library and closed the door. "What is it, Mrs. Birdwhistle?"

"I don't think we can do as you ask in the timeline stated on your list."

"What is needed to get the job done?"

"More people."

"Then hire more."

Mrs. Birdwhistle visibly relaxed. "Thank you, Miss. What shall I focus on first?"

"I think the kitchen. His Grace is giving a fete for the farmers in two weeks. We need to have the kitchen up and running at that time. He will give you a list of dishes he wants prepared for the occasion." Mona paused. "Mrs. Birdwhistle, are you all right? You seem pale. Shall I call for a doctor?"

"No, Miss. It's just the excitement is more than I am used to. The next few weeks will be full of hustle and bustle, but we shall do it. I was wondering how everyone is to be reimbursed. The helpers will be asking."

"Everyone will be paid in cash. You will give me a list of names and their duties. I will organize payment, which you will hand out after they sign their names on a register that they have received their money."

"Very good, Miss. Thank you." Mrs. Birdwhistle waited for Mona to dismiss her.

Mona started to speak, then hesitated.

"Is there something else, Miss?"

Deciding to broach the subject, Mona inquired, "Before you leave, I've been hearing stories about the Brynelleth ghosts. Can you enlighten me on the subject?"

"Fanciful talk from superstitious folks, Miss. Pay no heed."

"Have you ever seen a ghost in the manor, Mrs. Birdwhistle?"

Her face resembling chiseled stone, the housekeeper answered, "No, Miss. Never. Please excuse me. I must start planning the items on this list if we are to be done on time." The nervous twitch of her mouth gave her away. She gave a small nod and departed.

Left alone in the library, Mona pondered on why Mrs. Birdwhistle lied about seeing ghosts.

8

By the time Mona left Brynelleth at sunrise the next morning, the manor was buzzing with activity with more worker bees promising to arrive later that morning. She and three Pinkertons piled into a rented car and drove to the village. Once they arrived at the local inn, which also housed a pub, Mona said to the Pinkertons, "One of you go to the shop across the street. See if you can learn anything. I want you other two to go into the pub separately and yak with the locals. See if you can pick up any useful information."

"Yes, Miss Mona," they replied in unison.

Mona went into the pub first and asked if Mr. Nowak was in. She tried not to glance at customers already in the pub at this early hour. Several men were eating breakfast of fried eggs, baked beans, and sausage links. She couldn't wait until she got back to Brynelleth to have her breakfast. Her stomach was rumbling.

The middle-aged bartender with a scar over his left eye looked suspiciously at Mona. "Yes, Miss. I believe he is."

Mona, realizing that the scar was probably caused by shrapnel, made her tone more respectful, since this man was a Great War veteran. "Would you please tell him that Miss Moon from Brynelleth Manor is here to speak with him on behalf of the Duke?"

The bartender's eyes widened. "Yes, Miss."

"Is there a private room in which we may speak?"

"Yes, Miss." He turned to a barmaid. "Maisy, show Miss Moon to the Blue Luck room and then fetch Mr. Nowak."

"But that 'oom is for gentlemens only, sir."

"Do as I say, girl. Now vamoose," groused the bartender, rubbing his palms together. He turned to Mona. "May I get you anything, Miss?"

Mona was dying for a cup of tea, but made it a policy never to drink anything in public that was open. "No, thank you."

Maisy popped up beside Mona. "This way, Miss."

Mona followed her.

"You know women 're not allowed in this room. Tis for gentlmens."

"So I gathered. Is the room reserved for all gentlemen or only certain gentlemen?"

"Some club, they calls it. Only swells are allowed."

"Such as who?"

"I can't talk no more about it. I'll get into trouble with me boss." She paused before asking the next question. "Do you think the lads will go back to Brynelleth?"

"Which lads?"

"Them Polish lads."

"They lived at Brynelleth?"

"Yes, Miss, but of course, that was before the mischief happened."

"What mischief?"

"I shouldn't speak out of turn. It will get me in hot water with me boss."

Mona tried not to chuckle. Maisy was bursting at the seams to recount the story. Mona assured her, "I won't tell."

The young woman cagily looked about to see if anyone was listening. Whispering, she said, "It was due to them ghosts at Brynelleth. They've been stirring up awful. Tools missing, work sabotaged, strange cries in the night. That's why the Poles quit and moved here in the village. They were pushed out by the spirits. Souls of the dead are restless at Brynelleth."

Mona had learned one thing. Never allow Maisy to get a whiff of a secret or it would be all over the village in no time. The girl was a sponge that was easy to wring out.

Maisy unlocked a door and opened it for Mona. "There's a bell. Ring it if you need anything."

"Thank you, Maisy. You've been most helpful."

Maisy beamed, thinking Mona was nice. Usually, the upper class just barked orders at her. This woman seemed different.

Left alone, Mona got a handkerchief out of her purse and patted her forehead. Looking about the room, she was tempted to study the photographs hanging in rows on the dark panelled walls when Maisy returned with Mr. Nowak following.

Maisy curtsied and left, shutting the door.

Mr. Nowak waited for a few seconds and then furiously snatched open the door, checking the hallway. Grinning, he said with an Eastern European accent, "She would make for a marvelous spy. Maisy listens to every conversation and peeps into every keyhole."

Sitting at a dusty table, Mona studied Mr. Nowak. His white shirt was wrinkled as were his dark pants held up by suspenders. He hadn't bothered to shave nor comb his hair that day, but of course, it was still very early in the morning. Mona wondered if Maisy had to wake him.

"Do you know who I am?"

"You're the new Duke's American bird."

"I'm the woman who pays your upkeep. Why did you and your men walk off the job? You were hired to translate for the men and keep work on schedule."

"Something off is going on at the manor. Someone kept messin' with our work. The men and me figured we wait out here until the Duke could set things straight."

"You had a list of repairs that needed to be done and you were in charge of getting them done—and you were supposed to bunk at

Brynelleth—not run up a hotel bill in the village."

"Like I said—there was no point. Perhaps with a couple of more pounds per week, we could see our way back to the manor." Full of hubris, Nowak sat down and spread his legs wide with his muddy boot heels digging upright into the floor.

Mona disliked it when men sat so—that men thought nothing of displaying their crotches. Mona had dealt with men like Nowak before and was not going to negotiate. He thoroughly irritated her. Before he could speak, Mona announced, "This is what's going to happen, Mr. Nowak. If your men do not show up at Brynelleth by noon today, properly dressed, shaven, sober, and bathed, I will tear up your contract, but I will also stop payment on your rooms here and have you thrown out. Brynelleth will no longer pay for your upkeep or give references. Then I will sue each man under your supervision for breach of contract—including you. Any bar bills you all have accrued are yours to pay."

Awake to the fact that he had not intimidated Mona, Nowak sat up. "What about our back wages?"

"You will be paid a small stipend each week with the balance due when the work is completed to my satisfaction. You and your men will bunk at Brynelleth until the work is done. This free-loading off Brynelleth is finished. Show up ready to work or be thrown out into the streets on your bums."

Jumping up, Nowak shouted at Mona, "You are making slaves out of us! Me 'n the lads will not be treated this way."

"You agreed to a contract which is standard in England."

"You are nothing, but a tightfisted, rich American hellcat taking advantage of us poor Polish and Belgians."

Angry, Mona shot out of her seat. "I am Mona Moon. I do not take advantage of anyone nor do I take rubbish off men, who think they can bully me. I expect everyone to work and do their duty. Be at Brynelleth by noon today or be frozen out." Mona stormed out of the room. She tried to compose herself, but knew her face was beet red. She was mad. Really mad. With her platinum hair and yellow eyes, a red face made her look—well, frightening.

When Mona hurried back into the pub area, the bartender and Maisy were staring at her. Maisy's mouth hung open. The customers murmured quietly, becoming silent when they saw her glance at them. One man stood and took his cap off to her.

Mona guessed they had heard Nowak shouting or even the entire confrontation. She pulled the bartender aside and paid the workers' hotel bill, giving instructions that Brynelleth would no longer underwrite anyone's hotel or pub tabs after today.

The bartender happily accepted Mona's cash and didn't even blink when she asked for a receipt. He had not been pleased that Robert Farley was marrying an American, but now thought maybe Mona Moon was what Brynelleth required—new blood. The noble lines get watered down after so many generations. Too much inbreeding among the upper classes.

Yes, maybe Mona Moon was the angel they needed and not the devil they had feared.

9

Mona rushed back to Brynelleth and changed into trousers and an old tattered shirt. She was, at last, eating breakfast before she headed out to survey the estate and its farms. Robert wanted a complete check on the property boundaries.

Great Britain still maintained land under a feudal system. Everything and everyone's income revolved around the great manor houses. Families did not own the land, but worked the same farms for generations, paying rent to their manor lord, who actually owned the land—thus creating the landed gentry class. This system was becoming more untenable as aristocratic families could not afford to maintain such large dwellings when the price of crops fell, forcing their farmers to renege on their rents, and those in domestic service demanded better pay, more time off, and better working conditions. Many country manor houses were being sold and torn down while the land was auctioned off to pay off debts.

In the United States, families owned their own farms and ranches. However, families were being evicted from their farms by the banks when they defaulted on their mortgages. Again, the price of crops had dropped precipitously. It didn't help that the Midwest was experiencing a drought, and the topsoil was blowing away with the wind. This was causing a great exodus of farmers from the Plains states.

Mona was determined this was not going to happen to Mooncrest Farm or the Duchy of Brynelleth. First, Robert needed to get a legal grasp of his property boundaries. His deeds had descriptions like the border between his land and his neighbor's was divided by the rock fence and ended at the oak tree. Often these types of descriptions were useless during a dispute as the rock walls had been torn down for reuse or the majestic oak tree had been struck by lightning. Robert needed a new plat map with precise measurements. Since map making had been

Mona's vocation, the job fell to her.

She was putting jam on her toast when Robert strode into the dining room.

"Good morning, darling. You're up early." Robert bent over and kissed Mona on the lips. "Um, you taste like strawberry jam. Give me another smooch."

Mona held up her toast. "If you keep kissing me, I'll never get a start on those property lines."

"Killjoy." Robert poured himself a cup of coffee. "I heard you went into the village early this morning."

Surprised, Mona quit munching her breakfast. "Goodness, news travels fast. I guess the villagers think I'm horrid."

"On the contrary, they have a new respect for you. Nowak owes everyone in the village and is considered a bully. They were happy you gave him a dressing down."

"Well, that's good—I think."

"Are they going to finish the repairs?"

"Don't know. I gave Nowak an ultimatum though. Show up or be thrown out on your arse."

Although Robert thought seeing Mona's dander up was amusing, he didn't reply. It was one of the situations that no matter what he said, it would be wrong. He had enough experience with women to know better. Robert dished himself some eggs, baked beans, sausage, bacon, and grilled tomatoes from the buffet onto his plate.

"Are you going to eat all of that?" Mona asked.

"Busy morning. Won't be back for lunch."

"What will you be doing?"

"The annual counting of the sheep."

"I won't be back for lunch either. Going to survey the west side of the estate."

Robert nodded as he dove into his breakfast. He was hungry. "Good. Good. Need to get those boundaries up to modern legal standards."

"Robert?"

"Yes," he murmured between bites.

"Do you have ghosts at Brynelleth?"

Robert put down his fork and knife. "What an odd question? Where did you hear about our ghosts?"

"So you do have haints?"

"Nonsense uttered by frightened house maids. I've never seen one."

"Nowak said his men walked off because of

lack of pay, but the barmaid told me the workers complained of being haunted—missing tools, strange noises, seeing apparitions. That's the real reason they went to stay in the village hotel."

"A barmaid? See what I mean. Girls in these parts are impressionable. Pay no heed to these stories."

"The Pinkertons have reported that they have seen some strange things the night before as well. Is it possible that a stranger could be hiding in Brynelleth and not be detected? I mean the house is so large with so many unused rooms, it would be easy to hide."

Robert seemed concerned. "It's not without possibility, I guess." He looked at his watch. "Darling, can we discuss this over tea? I should be back by four."

"Of course. I've got to get a move on as well."

Robert pushed away his plate and got up. Kissing the top of Mona's head, Robert said, "Chin, chin," and strode out of the dining room.

Mona finished her breakfast while pondering if someone was hiding on the estate. Perhaps on the very floor as her bedroom. Thank goodness she had the locks changed. Little did Mona know that at that very moment, someone was now rifling through her belongings and papers in her bedroom.

But she would know—and very soon.

10

Mona and a Pinkerton had finished surveying the first section of Brynelleth's western border. In the distance one could see the sea. Mona breathed deeply. "I love the sea air," she said. "Nothing like it for the lungs."

"If you say so, Miss," the Pinkerton replied, looking at his watch. He was one of the younger Pinkertons and the most agreeable one. "This is a good spot for some lunch."

Mona watched him take the picnic basket out of the car and spread a blanket on the ground. From the hilltop where the two sat, they could see the chimneys of the manor. "It's lovely here. So unlike Kentucky."

"Are you saying Kentucky is not lovely, Miss Moon?"

"Kentucky is a different type of pretty. Know what I mean?" Mona watched the Pinkerton take out the sandwiches and hand her several soda pop bottles. He pulled out a thermos filled with coffee for himself.

Mona picked up a sandwich stuffed with thick slices of turkey.

"Wish this sandwich had a little mayo on it. Awfully dry," the Pinkerton said.

Mona peered into the basket and pulled out small bottles topped with wax paper and tied with string. "Here you go," she said, sniffing the contents. "Butter and mayo."

The Pinkerton fumbled around the basket, pulling out a small knife and two pieces of cherry pie. "Things are looking up." He and Mona slathered butter on their sandwiches as the mayonnaise was starting to separate.

"Thank you for volunteering to help me," Mona said, trying not to stare at the Pinkerton's gun holster.

"Anything to get out of window cleaning duty."

Mona laughed. "I think you all are good sports to do double duty. I don't think you signed up for scrubbing floors of a run-down manor."

"Miss, if you want my advice, sell Brynelleth. It's nothing more than a pile of tumbling bricks and stones."

"I can't. I'm going to marry His Grace and Brynelleth is his ancestral home. Too many people rely on Brynelleth for us to cut and run."

"I didn't mean to speak out of turn. It's just that Moon Manor is so elegant and modern. It makes Brynelleth look like a . . ." He stopped short.

"A dump?"

The Pinkerton nodded his head. "I must be out of my head talking like this. Please don't fire me."

"I don't take offense. You're very young yet. There are some responsibilities from which one can't walk away." She reached over. "Enough talk about Brynelleth. Hand me that piece of pie. I'm still hungry."

"My name is Charlie, by the way."

"Yes, I know. You're the one with a small crush on Miss Violet."

Blushing, Charlie changed the subject. "What's next?"

"Continue on and work until three. Then go back to Brynelleth for tea time."

"Afternoon tea is something I could get used to. Mrs. Wicket is awfully good at feeding us all sorts of cakes and biscuits. It's hard remembering to call cookies 'biscuits', but she gets cross if I don't. Tea time is something I'll miss back in the States."

Mona heard a hawk cry and scanned the sky searching until she spotted a flare of light flashing from one of the hills. "Did you see that?" Mona asked startled.

"What?"

"A flash. Reflection from a mirror, maybe. Over there. To your right."

The Pinkerton nonchalantly swiveled and picked up another sandwich while scrutinizing the hills. "I see it. I see it. Please act normally."

"Someone is watching us with binoculars."

"Either that or they are aiming a rifle with a scope at us," Charlie cautioned. "This makes me uncomfortable. I think we need to leave. Immediately!"

"Perhaps it is someone birdwatching," Mona said.

"Perhaps it is someone carrying through the death threats being sent to you."

Mona gasped.

"What? You didn't think we knew about them. We've been trying to chase their origins for weeks now."

"We'll discuss the threats later. What do you want me to do now?"

"I want you to rush into the car and lie down on the back seat. Don't pop your head up until I tell you to. On the count of three—run. One, two, three!"

The sound of a rifle reverberated off the hills creating an echo. PING! PING! Small bits of dirt flew up beside them.

Mona and Charlie made a dash for the car with Mona sliding into the back seat. Charlie, luckily having left the keys in the ignition, started the car moving even before he slammed his door shut. He turned onto a dirt road that rambled into the dense woods. Driving several hundred feet into the deep forest, Charlie slammed on the brakes.

"Why are you stopping?" Mona cried out from the floor of the back seat.

"There's a person lying the road! He looks hurt."

"It could be a trap."

Charlie replied, "Let me check. He could be really injured."

Both Mona and Charlie jumped out of the car and hurried over to the man sprawled on the ground. Charlie drew his gun while Mona knelt beside the man. She gently turned him over and said, "Oh, goodness." There was blood covering the man's chest.

"Is he alive?"

"Yes, but barely." Mona tore open the victim's shirt, discovering several bleeding wounds. "Get my coat out of the car. I'll use it to put pressure on his wounds."

Charlie retrieved Mona's coat while searching the woods. "We need to get out of here."

"I'll sit in the back with him."

Charlie tore the bottom of his shirt and wrapped the cloth around the man's torso. "This will help better. I'll get him into the car and then you can put pressure using the coat."

"Let's hurry. He's lost a lot of blood."

Suddenly the stranger's eyes fluttered open

and he grabbed Mona's hand. Using what strength he had left, the dying man uttered, "Le Puma. Le Puma. William Donovan. See William Donovan." He took one final gasp as his hand slipped slowly from Mona's.

Looking quite shocked, Charlie asked, "Is he dead?"

Mona placed her hand on the man's bloody chest and then her fingers on his wrist. "I think so. I can't feel a pulse." She gently closed the man's eyes. "I think he's gone, Charlie." She searched his pockets, finding an army knife and twenty-five pounds in his wallet, but no ID or family pictures.

Charlie searched the man's knapsack and found a loaded revolver, a half-empty thermos, a map of the area, compass, two ham sandwiches, and binoculars. "Help me, Miss Moon."

Mona helped set the body up while Charlie tugged at the clothes to find any labels, but they had all been cut out. She looked at the Pinkerton. "Nothing, Charlie, not a single clue except that he spoke with an American accent, was not an observant Jew or Muslim, and did not carry his passport."

Charlie looked at the man's hands. "No sign of manual labor on these hands, but they are strong. No cuts, scars, bruises, calluses, warts—nothing."

"He's well groomed. Look at the back of his neck. It's been shaven." Mona took a sniff of the man's hair. "Hair cologne. He got a haircut recently and his nails are manicured."

Charlie glanced down the path. "We need to get out of here. Whoever shot at us may be coming." Charlie dragged the body to the car and Mona helped lift it into the back seat. After the stranger was situated, Mona covered him with her coat. Anxious, Charlie and Mona glanced awkwardly at each other for a moment. This was not the afternoon they had expected. Climbing in the car, Mona pulled a gun from her knapsack while Charlie tucked his gun back in his holster. As Charlie drove back to Brynelleth, Mona looked out the rear window. They both were silent, trying to process the afternoon's violent events. After twenty daunting minutes, Charlie pulled up to a side door of Brynelleth.

He asked, "Will you be all right?"

"I'll be fine. Notify the rest of the boys, but

keep this as quiet as possible. Don't say anything to His Grace. I'll inform him. It is His Grace's duty to call the authorities."

Charlie glanced back at the corpse. "What did he mean by Le Puma?"

"It's French for cougar."

"That's odd."

"I don't think he was talking about a cat. I think he was telling me about a person."

"Who is William Donovan?"

Mona looked at Charlie. "The less you know about William Donovan, the better. In fact, just forget you ever heard that name. Now gather the rest of the Pinkertons. We've got to get a handle on this mess before the constable is called."

That's when Charlie knew Mona Moon was hiding something and she was worried. That made him worry. What secret was Mona guarding?

And who was William Donovan?

11

Robert bypassed informing the local village constable and called MI5, mentioning William Donovan. Afterward, Mr. Mott and Charlie secretly deposited the body in the ice house. That evening, two men showed up at the manor, declaring they had an appointment with Robert Farley, Duke of Brynelleth.

Mrs. Birdwhistle thought this odd as it was close to dinner time. Finch had all ready rung the dinner gong. Who makes an appointment that late in the evening? To top it off, Mona interceded and showed the gentlemen out to the garden with His Grace following. The four sat at a table with their backs to the manor and spoke in low tones.

Twenty minutes later, Mona and one of the

gentlemen left the group and reentered the house. She found Finch and instructed all the staff to assemble in the great hall—including Mr. Nowak and the foreign laborers who had straggled back to Brynelleth. Mona and the gentleman stood by the front door along with three of the Pinkertons while the other guards rounded up all the employees except for Violet.

Once everyone was collected, Mona said, "I'm sorry to take you away from your duties and cause dinner to be delayed, but something rather important has turned up, and His Grace thinks everyone should be informed." She turned to the man standing beside her. "This gentleman is Ethan McTavish from Scotland Yard. His Grace called Scotland Yard because someone took a pot shot at me while I was surveying the western border."

The entire staff stirred and glanced at each other.

"Luckily, I was not hurt."

"It could have been a poacher, Miss," Finch said. "We have trouble with them from time to time. If we let them, they'd hunt the wildlife out of Brynelleth. It causes them to have hard feelings when we put a stop to their shenanigans. They like to give us a scare once in a while."

"A possibility, but the shot was a little too close for comfort."

Bertha offered, "It could have been someone from the village who is anti-American."

Mrs. Wicket told Bertha to shush and gave her an angry look.

"That is not all. When I returned to my suite, my suite had been searched and some business papers stolen. And that is with a new lock on the door. To me that is desecrating the late Duchess' room."

The staff murmured and nodded slightly amongst themselves. They agreed with Mona as they adored their late mistress.

Mona continued, "Mr. McTavish and his assistant will question everyone. It is important you tell Mr. McTavish anything you might deem suspicious. We expect everyone to cooperate."

"It's Chief Inspector McTavish, Miss."

"I'm so sorry, Chief Inspector. Please forgive me."

"It's all right, Miss. I understand Americans don't put much stock into titles."

Finch asked, "What about dinner for His Grace and you?"

Mona patted him on his shoulder. "It will be fine, Finch. His Grace and I will fend for ourselves." She addressed the entire staff, "Once you have been questioned, you may return to your duties. No one is to leave this room until Chief Inspector McTavish says you may. That is all. Thank you."

Chief Inspector McTavish's assistant came from the kitchen and nodded to him. Robert, Charles, and Violet followed him. Seeing the staff was upset, Robert assured them that it was fine and to answer questions as honestly as possible.

"I'd like to start with Bertha, please," the Chief Inspector requested, looking at the staff list.

"Why me? Why me?" Bertha asked, looking frantically around. "I didn't mean nothing about people not liking Americans. Just idle gossip."

Using a stern voice, Robert said, "Go with the Chief Inspector like a good lass, Bertha. Use the library. Show McTavish where it is."

Slumping her shoulders, Bertha acquiesced. "Yes, Your Grace. Follow me, sirs."

Relieved that McTavish and the Pinkertons were taking control of the situation, Mona, Violet, and Robert went into the butler's pantry where the dinner had been set out as the kitchen had been dismantled for the remodeling. Dinner was Shepherd's Pie and Yorkshire pudding. They filled their plates and went into the dining room to eat where they sat silently while spooning food into their mouths.

Mona was so upset she could hardly taste the food. "Robert, is the man—?"

Robert shook his head. "Not now. We'll talk later."

Violet offered, "I have something to share with the two of you."

Robert said, "I know, but it will have to wait until the servants have gone to bed. Just hang tight. We are playing a dangerous game here."

Violet sat back in her chair, pushing her plate away. "I'm not hungry. May I be excused?"

"Of course, dear," Mona said. "I'll be up shortly myself."

After Violet left, Mona grabbed Robert's hand. "Are you sure you want to marry me?"

"This may have nothing to do with you."

"You know it does, darling. I'm bringing trouble to your door."

Robert pushed his plate away also. "I'm not hungry either. I think I'll go sit in on the interviews." He rose and after kissing Mona's cheek, left the dining room.

Left alone in the vast chamber and feeling unsettled herself, Mona folded her napkin and left for her suite. Once there, she called to Violet, who came out of her bedroom. "What was it you wanted to tell us, Violet?"

Violet whispered, "The dead man in the ice cellar."

"Yes?"

"I was the lookout when we removed the body from the ice house. Your coat fell off the poor man's face while we were loading him into the trunk of McTavish's car. I got a good look, and it was the same man who almost pushed me off the ship's gangplank. Remember when His Grace had to pull me out of the way when we were disembarking?"

"You're sure?"

"Positive. It was the same man."

Their discussion was interrupted by a knock

on the door. Violet cautiously opened it with Mona holding a gun on the door.

"Put that blasted thing away," groused Robert.

Mona quickly put the revolver in her purse. "Sorry, Robert."

"Everyone is downstairs, so I think it is safe to talk without being overheard."

"What's happening?" Mona asked.

"From the interviews I sat in on, there has been mischief here. It was as you reported, Mona—strange noises, tools missing, and other silly whatnot. There may indeed be someone hiding on the premises just as you thought. What I'm really concerned about is that your room was searched and papers are missing, not to mention your being shot at."

Mona concurred, "Whoever is creating this crisis knows how to pick locks or has the power to walk through walls. It makes me feel very unsafe in my very own bedroom. Also Violet says the dead man is the same person who almost pushed her into the sea as we were coming down the ship's ramp at Plymouth."

Robert turned to Violet. "Are you sure, Violet?"

"I am, Your Grace."

"Robert, is the staff believing our cover story that McTavish is from Scotland Yard?" Mona asked.

"I believe so. He and his partner are really from MI5."

"And the body?" Mona knew where the body was, but just wanted to be reassured by Robert. She felt uneasy and skittish.

"We put him in the boot of McTavish's car. He'll take the body with him. The man's death will be kept quiet. The local authorities will not be informed."

"How did he die?" Mona asked. "I couldn't be sure. There was so much blood."

"He was stabbed, unlucky fellow."

"That's awful," Violet said. "He looked very young."

"It seems someone wishes to cause us harm," Robert said. "And we have another problem coming up this weekend."

"What's that?"

"Viscountess Thelma Furness has asked us to spend the weekend at her estate. She wants to officially announce our engagement. I don't want to offend Thelma as she is the mistress of the Prince of Wales, but I really can't stand the woman."

"Isn't she the twin sister of Gloria Vanderbilt, who is having a custody battle over her daughter?" Mona asked.

Animated, Violet said, "I read about it in the papers. They call the custody battle the *trial of the century*. It's the little girl's aunt who is suing the mother. Says the mother is morally unfit and spending too much of the little girl's inheritance."

Mona cocked her head to one side, studying Robert's expression. "So you were putting her off. How long have you had the invitation?"

Robert grimaced. "I guess I delayed giving an answer, but McTavish says we should attend the party. Act as if everything is normal. Says he'll have men there. What say you? We won't go if you don't wish so."

"We should, but only if I can bring two Pinkertons and Violet with me. Perhaps our nemesis will be there. I'd like to ferret him out."

"Who says it's a *he*?" Violet asked.

"You're quite right, Violet," Mona said. "And there could be more than one of them."

"Let's not forget why we are here, ladies. It's to restore Brynelleth back to her former glory."

Mona replied, "It's surprising you refer to Brynelleth as female. The manor comes across to me as male, but you are quite right. We are here to work, regardless of the obstacles." Mona gave Robert a reassuring hug and teased, "Aside from murder and mayhem, we are making headway. All the linens have been repaired. The staff has new uniforms and aprons thanks to Violet. The kitchen will be refitted and painted this week. Most of the downstairs has been cleaned and scrubbed. The staff will start on the upstairs next week. Pea gravel has been ordered to repair the driveway, and Mr. Nowak has assured me that he can fix the fountain and the roof."

"How is it working out with our Polish immigrants?" Robert asked.

"I was told that they slunk in around one o'clock, and Mrs. Birdwhistle assigned their rooms. As soon as they put their kits up, they went to work on the roof."

Robert reached for his sterling cigarette case and, remembering Mona disliked the smoke, put it back in his coat pocket. "This is so ridiculous.

We should be in Monte Carlo having the time of our lives instead of having to deal with this muck."

"We will have a lifetime of pleasure. We just need to tidy up a few things first."

Glad to put the discussion of the dead man behind them, Robert asked, "How's the inventory going?"

"Mrs. Rymer and one of the Pinkertons with an accounting background are working on the list together."

Violet piped up, "I'm helping when I have time."

"That's good."

Mona asked, "How's the estate coming along?"

"I've got both lady farmers using the tractors, and I've heard talk that the men are noticing. Everyone on the estate has been invited to a tea weekend after next. I've hired local lads to play music, and Mrs. Wicket is planning the menu. I told her to keep it simple. Food you can eat with your fingers—that sort of thing. You won't have to do a thing. This is my shindig."

"I'd better have Mrs. Wicket order more flour

and sugar," Mona mused.

"Mrs. Wicket has everything under control. She is hiring out just in case the kitchen is not finished in time."

"Well, then, I'll concentrate on the manor. I think I'd better put off surveying for now."

Robert kidded, "You think?"

"There is only one thing to do. Call up Viscountess Furness tomorrow and say that we would be pleased to be the guests of honor at her soiree."

"I'll call first thing tomorrow morning." Robert looked at his watch. "Ladies, I think you should call it a night. Please pull that bureau against the door when I leave."

Violet said, "You better believe we will."

"I'll stay with the MI5 agents until they leave and lock up. You two get some rest. I'll see you both in the morning."

Violet swept off to her room, giving the engaged couple privacy. She didn't know how Mona felt about spending two days at Viscountess Furness' estate, but she was looking forward to the visit. She needed a break from the constant work, and a weekend in the country sounded grand. To make it even more special, she would ask Mona to assign Charlie as one of her body-guards. He had caught Violet's eye and what would be a more perfect way to explore romance than at a weekend party!

12

"May I introduce my fiancée, Madeline Mona Moon," Robert said, kissing the cheek of Viscountess Thelma Furness. "This is wonderful of you to throw a party in our honor."

Thelma returned Robert's kiss and turned her attention to Mona. She was startled by Mona's stark white hair, alabaster skin, and light amber eyes, even though she had been warned of Mona's unusual coloring. Recovering quickly, Thelma said, "I've heard quite a good deal about you, my dear. You're the only woman who's been able to snag our Robert on a permanent basis." She gave Robert a little push. "He's been such a naughty boy. Half the women here shall weep into their pillows tonight."

"Just half?" Mona asked.

Surprised that Mona was not insulted by her poke about Robert's past romances, Lady Thelma burst out laughing. "Oh, my dear, we are going to get along famously."

"It's very nice to meet you, Lady Furness," Mona replied. "I hope we can be great friends."

"Call me Thelma," the Viscountess said, pronouncing Thelma with a hard t similar to the Spanish pronunciation. "I'm an American like you."

"Thank you."

"You must come and meet my other guests. They're out on the patio sunning themselves. Come. Come."

Robert interceded, "It's been a long drive, Thelma. Mona might like to freshen up before your guests try to devour her."

"Nonsense, Mona looks fabulous just as she is. Wonderful idea dressing all in white, my dear. Makes you look so virginal."

"Or like a sacrificial lamb? Why do I feel I'm about to be consumed by wolves?"

Thelma replied, "I doubt anyone would get the better of you, Miss Moon." Thelma put her arm around Mona's shoulders as she walked her out. "Be hearty, mi'lass. You'll need strong shoulders and constitution for the British upper class. They can be devastatingly cruel with those they consider socially inferior."

"And an heiress from Kentucky is inferior?"

"My advice is to go for the jugular before they do. Trust me. From one countrywoman to another—strike and draw first blood or the wolf pack with pounce en masse." They walked through a large parlor and stepped out onto a patio that had a vista of a park that stretched over the small rolling hills and finally ended at a distant shimmering lake crowned by a plume of water arching high above its surface.

"Look, everyone. Look who I have with me. The guests of honor have arrived."

A few of the men rose to shake Robert's hand and greet his intended bride.

Thelma said, "Mona, I'd like you to meet my twin sister, Gloria."

Mona nodded at the attractive, but droopy-looking woman. "Very nice to meet you." Mona made sure she did not mention the lawsuit Gloria was still waging for the custody of her daughter against the girl's aunt, Gertrude Vanderbilt Whitney.

"And I believe you know Herr Ribbentrop."

Mona turned to face Ribbentrop. "Yes, we traveled on the same ship together. How are you?"

"Better now that I am once again in the presence of the beautiful Mona Moon." He bowed his head, clicking his heels.

"So this is the country estate you were visiting." Mona stated.

"Yes, I did not lie."

"I never said you did," Mona replied, cooly.

"Your Grace," Herr Ribbentrop said, greeting Robert.

Robert nodded, obviously displeased to see the man again.

Smiling broadly, Ribbentrop ignored Robert's slight.

"And this is my good friend, Wallis Simpson," Thelma announced.

A petite dark-haired woman dressed in the latest French fashion gave Mona the once-over. "A pleasure to meet another American among this dreary sea of impoverished British aristocrats."

Thelma admonished, "Be nice, Wallis. Mona

might not approve of your sarcastic humor as she is marrying an impoverished British aristocrat."

Mona took an immediate dislike to Wallis Simpson.

Wallis looked at Robert. "So sorry. Didn't mean to be offensive."

"But you did mean to be, my dear," Ribbentrop said in a false falsetto voice, derision rippling through his unwavering smile.

"Oh, shut up, Joachim," Wallis retorted, using Ribbentrop's first name.

Thelma leaned over and whispered to Mona. "See what I mean about drawing first blood."

Mona replied, "It only matters if I care, which I don't."

Ribbentrop laughed. "See there, Wallis. You have competition. You might not be the only favorite American of the month. Miss Moon might take your place in you-know-who's affection."

"You can be such a bore, Joachim," Wallis said, pouting.

"Yes, Joachim," Thelma said. "Both of you be nice."

"You have such beautiful grounds," Mona

observed, wanting to change the direction of the conversation.

Pleased, Thelma said, "You must see my gardens. They are simply divine, but wait. I have a surprise for you."

A raven-haired woman stepped out from a summer house and rushed toward Mona. "Mona! Mona!"

Mona looked up in surprise. "Alice! Oh, my gosh. So splendid to see you here."

Lady Alice Morrell Nithercott, Mona's great friend, hugged Mona tightly. "So good to see you as well. I can't wait to hear all your news. I know you've been frightfully busy with Brynelleth. I know I was to come to Brynelleth last week, but we had to cancel. I'll tell you about it later."

Alice's husband, Professor Ogden Nithercott, strolled behind and stopped by Robert. They shook hands hardily. "So good to see you, mate. Looking good, Robert. The States agree with you."

"Mona agrees with me."

"Let's all have a drink," Thelma suggested. She beckoned to a footman.

Mona spoke up. "You must excuse me. It was

a long drive from Brynelleth, and I must look a fright. I'd like to freshen up. May someone show me to my room?"

"I will," Alice twittered. "You are sandwiched in between our room and Robert's."

Mona raised an eyebrow. "How convenient."

Alice smiled ingratiatingly at the group. "Please excuse us. I need to powder my nose as well."

The Viscountess said, "Of course, dears. Don't forget tea is at five in the main drawing room, and the party starts at nine. Society reporters will be attending, so look your very best."

"We'll be present for tea," Mona promised as she and Alice ventured into the house. Realizing all eyes were upon her, Mona hurried up the main staircase with Alice leading the way.

When they reached the second landing, Alice hurried to the third door on the left side of the staircase. "Here is your room," Alice said, trying the doorknob. "It's locked."

"Good. Violet must be inside." Mona gave three slow taps and the two rapid ones.

Violet opened the door and spoke sharply.

"Where have you been?"

Mona laughed. "Meeting the inmates." She and Lady Alice entered the room and locked the door behind them.

"Golly, Lady Alice." Violet hugged her. "So wonderful to see you."

"Likewise, Violet." Alice held her at arms' length and twirled her around. "You have grown so, I hardly recognized you. A young lady you are now."

Violet giggled.

Mona threw down her purse and gloves. "Have the Pinkertons searched the room?"

"Yes, they even tapped on the walls for secret panels."

"Secret panels?"

Violet said, "You know—hidden doors that lead to tunnels. All these old houses have secret passageways and priests' holes."

"Like at my house, Mona," Lady Alice said, agreeing with Violet.

"Yes, Miss Mona."

"You know I never thought about secret doors at Breynelleth," Mona said, nodding.

"Brynelleth has them," Lady Alice replied.

Thinking she needed to concentrate on her current domicile, Mona said, "Hmm. What about the key to the door?"

Violet replied, "Here it is, but the housekeeper has one also and she wouldn't give it up either. I've already tried."

"Any connecting doors?"

"Yes, one that leads to His Grace's room, but it's locked."

"Lady Furness thinks of everything," Mona said, amused.

"Not always. She doesn't follow the consequences of her actions," Lady Alice said.

"Whatever do you mean?"

"You've met Wallis Simpson?"

"Yes," Mona answered.

"Who is Wallis Simpson?" Violet asked, looking between Mona and Alice.

Alice said to Mona, "Notice the tension between Thelma and Wallis?"

"That's not their normal behavior?"

"Not since the Prince of Wales started paying attention to Wallis instead of the Viscountess."

"Who is Wallis Simpson?" Violet asked again.

"A rich American twice divorced," Lady Alice

said, "with her eye on becoming the Prince of Wales' next main squeeze."

"What does she mean?" Violet asked, glancing at Mona.

"It means the future king of England is swapping mistresses," Mona said, taking off her white jacket. Violet took it and hung it up.

Alice leaned in toward Mona. "Not totally yet, but Wallis is gaining ground and fast."

Violet's mouth gaped open. "You mean the Prince of Wales has mistresses and everyone knows?"

Lady Alice playfully threw a pillow at Violet's head, saying to Mona. "I thought you taught this girl the facts of life."

Mona replied, "She knows how the bees and the birds work. It's just that Violet has a higher moral compass. She is shocked by the tawdry."

"I'm right here," Violet complained. "I can hear you both."

Lady Alice lay on the bed. "I'm afraid our Prince takes after his grandfather, Edward VII. Now there was a womanizer."

"I understand his queen invited Edward VII's last mistress to his bedside as he lay dying," Mona said, looking out the window.

"That's a very understanding wife," Alice joked.

Mona could see Robert and Ogden were speaking with the Pinkertons. Out from the corner of the patio strolled Ribbentrop smoking a cigarette while watching them.

As Mona was watching Ribbentrop, Wallis Simpson joined him. As they began to converse, Mona gently opened her window to eavesdrop.

"What are you doing, Mona?" Lady Alice asked.

Mona waved her off. "Shush!"

Lady Alice climbed off the bed and tiptoed to the window, peering out. "Oh, it's just those two."

Violet joined the ladies. "Who are you looking at?" Not being able to see over their shoulders, she gave a little nudge, pushing them to the left. Leaning out the window, Violet drew her head back in quickly. Then she took another peek, gasped, and quickly closed the window.

Mona asked, "What's the matter, Violet? Your face is flushed."

"Remember that lady I saw with Ribbentrop

at the Savoy giving him a pack of letters?"

"Of course, I do."

"Well, that's the same lady with him now."

"Are you sure?" Mona asked.

"I'm positive," Violet swore. "I'd know her as if she climbed out of my bowl of soup."

Mona felt fear creep up her spine. Why was an American socialite hobnobbing with a Nazi, and whose letters did she give to Ribbentrop?

13

The musicians were playing an old fashion waltz when Robert escorted Mona down the staircase. It was five minutes before nine in the evening and they were to join the Viscountess at the receiving line. Guests were arriving early and asking Thelma where the American upstart was. Hearing comments about herself, Mona plastered on a smile, knowing she was going to have to win these aristocrats over.

Robert squeezed her hand and shot her a winsome smile.

"Now I know how the early Christians felt," Mona murmured.

"Shall we face the lions together, my dear?"

A pool of photographers rushed the couple making their way down the staircase. "Look here,

Miss Moon. Duke, smile. Over here, Miss. Hold it. Fine. That's tickity-boo."

Robert and Mona paused and posed for the photographers. After several minutes, Robert said, "Wrap it up, boys. Thank you."

Gobsmacked at the dress Mona was wearing, the Viscountess walked over and grabbed Mona's hands. "My dear. You look absolutely stunning. Every man here tonight is going to fall in love with you. Robert, have you ever seen a woman look so magnificent?"

"Mona always has appeared like a goddess to me."

"Mona, you are a glittering delight."

"Thank you, Thelma. I've been saving this dress for our engagement announcement. You have given me a grand occasion to wear it." Mona was wearing a silvery chiffon dress with pleated lines of crystals in parallel with each other the entire length of the dress. The Grecian design of the sleeveless dress was a simple front and back panels sewn up both sides allowing a neck and arm holes. It was cinched at the waist with a crystal encrusted belt. When Mona walked, light shimmered from the dress.

"My goodness, Mona, you look like a twinkling silver torch," greeted Professor Ogden Nithercott, kissing her cheek.

Lady Alice elbowed her husband out of the way. "What my charming husband means to say is that you look stunning, my dear."

"I said that, didn't I?" Ogden replied, confused.

Mona gave him a grateful smile. "Thank you, Ogden. I accept the compliment."

Robert slapped his great friend on the back. "I've never understood women either, Ogden."

The Viscountess said, "Let's take our places, please."

Robert and Mona stood to the left of the Viscountess. As people were announced by the head butler, Thelma greeted them, introduced them to Robert who then introduced Mona to them. Fortunately, Robert knew most of the guests and greeted them heartily. He hadn't seen many of them since before the Great War and enjoyed seeing his old friends and comrades again.

Mona loved observing Robert so jovial and relaxed. She saw a glimpse of what Robert was like before the War. He must have been a dashing youth—handsome, chivalrous, charming, and unsullied. Everything so desired in English manhood—a Dorian Gray before he meets Lord Henry Wotton.

After standing and greeting people for fifteen minutes, Mona heard, "Well, Miss Moon, we meet again."

Mona looked away from Robert and stared into the face of William Donovan, President Roosevelt's gentleman spy. "Mr. Donovan, I didn't see you enter."

Ignoring Mona's remark, he said, "You look very stunning, Miss Moon."

"Thank you."

Leaning in close as if to give her a peck on the cheek, Donovan whispered, "Meet me in the garden about an hour from now." He pulled away and gave Mona a big smile. "I understand congratulations are in order."

Mona murmured, "I don't know if I can get away."

Smiling, Donovan lowered his voice again. "His Grace and you are in grave danger. Must speak with you."

Grabbing Donovan's hand and shaking it

warmly, Mona said out loud, "Thank you for coming. Hope to speak with you later." Mona returned to greeting the Viscountess' guests until ten. Exhausted from shaking hands and smiling, Mona begged off, saying she needed some air.

"We're finished here anyway," Thelma replied. "I think everyone has arrived that is going to come. Let's join our guests."

Robert asked the Viscountess, "May I have this dance?"

Pleased, Thelma smiled and held out her hand for Robert to escort her to the dance floor.

That gave Mona the chance to slip out into the garden. Motioning to Lady Alice to join her, the two sauntered arm-in-arm into the garden—just two friends enjoying the evening air. They passed the British fascist Oswald Mosley heatedly arguing with a fat, bald man about politics. Behind the two, stood gentlemen of all ilks and persuasions, listening to the discussion. The older man, smoking a foul cigar, looked up briefly as the ladies walked past and gave Mona a hard look.

His stare gave Mona the willies as he seemed to be taking great note of her. Mona asked, "Who is the man with Mosley? I forgot his name."

"That is Winston Churchill. His mother was American, you know. He wants to be Prime Minister, but he won't be voted in. He's had too many failures in his career and he's a blowhard. Besides, he's too old."

"I don't know why, but it seemed Mr. Churchill took a picture of me, but that is ridiculous as he didn't possess a camera. It was a foolish feeling on my part of being looked at and looked through."

"He claims to have a photographic memory. Next time he meets you, Mona, he will recollect you. I think he is a fool, but it is remarkable what the man remembers."

"What makes you think he is a fool?"

"Churchill keeps claiming that we will soon be at war with Germany if we don't stop placating Hitler. I can't think of any politician who would want to start another European war after the devastation of the last one—even Hitler. Everyone in Europe is anti-war and pro-peace."

Mona made a note to herself to remember Churchill. Something told her that she would run into him again.

Mona and Lady Alice ventured deep into the garden so as to be away from prying eyes. Deep within the green oasis and hidden from the ballroom guests by massive yew hedges, William Donovan stepped out from behind a tree. He nodded to Lady Alice and said to Mona, "Walk with me."

Lady Alice stood by the tree and kept watch.

"Has MI5 been in touch with you?" Mona asked.

"They have given me a full report. That gentleman whom you found was one of my agents. I had assigned him to keep watch over you."

"I'm so sorry." Mona was horrified. She felt sick to her stomach that such a young man was killed on her account.

Donovan remarked, "He must have seen something he shouldn't have. Poor boy."

"Was he able to report anything to you, Mr. Donovan?"

"He said you were being followed by an enemy agent, who had been recruited to put pressure on you to sell copper to Germany. The man has infiltrated Brynelleth. Your staff at Brynelleth is compromised. You and His Grace should trust no one."

"Is it Herr Ribbentrop? He keeps popping up."

"No, he said the man's code name was Le Puma, but he was trying to discover the man's real identity and said the agent wore disguises, making it harder to track him down. But my man was closing in on him."

"Your man mentioned the name Le Puma to me before he died. How did he discover the agent's code name?"

"He went through Ribbentrop's papers on the ship."

"Is Ribbentrop here because of me?"

"I think he is here on a fishing expedition. You are just one of many he's attempting to cultivate for the Third Reich. I wouldn't think he knows Le Puma's identity any more than we do. He just knows Le Puma is in the country."

"My companion, Violet, saw Ribbentrop with Wallis Simpson, who handed him a packet of letters at the Savoy."

Donovan's eyes flashed. "Ah, Mrs. Simpson. Did Miss Violet see who the letters were from?"

"No, but she said she could see a crest on the envelope."

"Too bad. That would have been useful information."

"A crest would suggest a person of rank—perhaps the Prince of Wales. I've heard tales of Simpson and the Prince becoming . . . close."

"It also could suggest hotel stationery. I know of several that have crests printed on their envelopes."

Sensing that Donovan didn't wish to discuss the Prince of Wales, but tucked that piece of information about the letters away, Mona segued, "You said my life and Robert's were in danger."

"You are. One of the things my man uncovered was that if you were not amenable to selling copper to the Third Reich, you were to be eliminated in favor of your aunt. That's why Le Puma is here."

"I see." Mona was not surprised.

"Even though your Pinkertons are good, they are not trained to handle international espionage. The German agent after you is a trained killer, probably a sniper from the Great War."

"What do you suggest?"

"Go home, Miss Mona. England is no place for you at the moment."

"I know that I'm no Mata Hari, but I am not a stranger to peril, Mr. Donovan."

"If you remember Hari was executed."

Mona did not respond.

"Let me be clear. The Duke of Brynelleth is vehemently anti-Hitler or fascism of any kind. His Grace is very vocal about this and is targeted for his beliefs. The Nazis do not want to see Brynelleth restored and will do their utmost to see your restoration plans fail, even if that means killing you or those around you. You must leave and go back to the States."

"So we should just cave into their threats?"

Before Donovan could respond, Lady Alice appeared and hissed, "Someone is coming."

Donovan pushed Mona toward Lady Alice and faded into the background.

Taking their cue, Mona and Lady Alice nonchalantly ambled back to the ball when they bumped into Gloria Vanderbilt.

"Oh, I didn't know anyone was taking the air besides me," Gloria said, taken aback seeing the two women.

"I needed a few moments away from all the prying and gossiping," Mona replied.

"I feel your pain," Gloria said, sadly. "I'm sorry to say that your engagement has taken the heat off me. That is to say I'm sorry for you, but relieved for me."

"I understand," Mona said, sympathetically. "Why don't you walk with us?"

"Actually, I was sent to find you. Thelma needs you back at the ball. She wants to make your engagement announcement."

"Of course. We'll hurry back immediately." Mona and Lady Alice rushed back to the manor with Gloria lagging behind. Upon entering the ballroom, Mona spied Robert and the Viscountess standing upon the staircase landing in the great foyer. Mona hurried to join them.

"Here she is," Thelma said gladly. "We thought we might have to send out a search party for you."

Robert stood by Mona and put his hand around her waist. She did likewise, smiling up at him.

"Friends, I have an announcement to make," Thelma said. "It is my great pleasure to reveal that His Grace, Duke of Brynelleth, Lawrence Robert Emerton Dagobert Farley has asked

Madeline Mona Moon to be his bride and mistress of Brynelleth. To our delight, Miss Moon has accepted His Grace's proposal and shall soon become Duchess of Brynelleth. Let me propose a toast to their happiness." Thelma took a flute of champagne from a waiter's tray. "Robert. Mona. We wish you both great joy on your journey together."

"Hear. Hear," the crowd murmured.

Mona and Robert beamed at each other as the crowd cheered. Robert pulled Mona close and kissed her.

Caressing Robert's face for a second, Mona said, "I guess you're stuck with me now."

"I wouldn't have it any other way, my American cow."

Bulbs flashed as Thelma, Robert, and Mona posed for pictures. Mona didn't mind posing for the newspapers at the moment, showing off her diamond and emerald engagement ring. As the cameras flared and bulb after flash bulb was ejected onto the floor, Mona smiled. In between bursts of flashes, she saw Ribbentrop and Wallis Simpson standing off to the side, scowling at her. Only when Ribbentrop saw Mona staring at him, did he nod his head in deference of her and smile. He said something to Simpson, so she smiled, too.

The fact that her marriage to Robert Farley displeased them both made Mona smile even wider. Mona had gone from being a broke cartographer to an heiress to a business woman to being the fiancée of a duke. Life couldn't get any better.

But Mona was to soon learn—the moment of one's triumph is when the Devil comes, and the Devil was on his way.

14

There was a crescendo of excited chatter as people stopped dancing and rushed into the grand foyer.

"What is everyone looking at?" Mona asked.

Robert let out a soft moan. "You didn't, Thelma?"

"I did. He hasn't seen you for years. Now Robert, don't be rude. I went to a great deal of trouble getting him here. He's supposed to be at a polo match."

"Whom are we discussing?" Mona asked, stretching her neck to see beyond the crowd.

"Oh, he must have arrived!" exclaimed Thelma, patting her face with her lace handkerchief.

Edward Albert Christian George Andrew Patrick David Windsor, Prince of Wales, commonly known as David entered the room with his entourage. The band played the Prince of Wales' favorite tune as he scattered the bowing and curtsying throng and strode over to where Mona and Robert stood.

Thelma curtsied.

Robert bowed, saying, "Your Royal Highness."

David clapped Robert on the back. "Too formal, cousin. Introduce me to this fascinating creature whom you are engaged to."

"May I introduce my fiancée, Madeline Mona Moon? This is His Royal Highness, the Prince of Wales."

The Prince turned to address Mona. "Egads, it's true what they say about you, Miss Moon. You are a vision of loveliness." He peered closely at her eyes. "I was told your eyes were yellow, but they are something to see."

As Mona was an American, she did not curtsy, but replied, "Thank you, Your Royal Highness. It's most kind of you to say so."

"It's not kind of me at all. It's the truth. Look around Miss Moon. Nothing but dull-looking brown chipping sparrows—every one of them, but you shine like the moon—like the stars in the sky."

"That's not nice, David," Thelma said, irritated that the Prince of Wales was insulting her guests.

"Was I being a boor?"

"Very much so. You've hurt my feelings."

"So sorry, old girl, but I don't feel like being nice tonight. I've had a horrible day and want something to go my way. Ah, that's lovely music your musicians are playing. Makes my feet want to have a patter of their own. They need to move—celebrate this auspicious occasion of Robert's engagement. I'm going to steal the intended bride away for a dance."

Mona realized that being seen dancing with the future king would guarantee an invitation from every aristocratic family in the United Kingdom—and invite gossip as well. The Prince of Wales was a known connoisseur of women. She decided to take the risk. "I'd be delighted. Shall we now?"

David looked astonished at Robert. "She didn't even ask your permission, Robert."

Robert replied, "American women have a

strong streak of independence, David, as you know."

David glanced knowingly at Thelma. "I know. I'm a whipping boy where beautiful dominant women are concerned."

Mona felt nauseated. Here was one of the most celebrated bachelors in all of Christendom. The Prince was handsome, educated, and a rascal—a charming rascal at that—and his people adored him for it. They winked at his romantic escapades and his pleasure seeking activities as they disliked his father's sour disposition and obsession with duty. After the Great War, people wanted to have fun. The Prince of Wales epitomized that sense of freedom of throwing off Victorian restrictions.

Thelma said, "Oh, David, you love being bossed around by beautiful women. When you're finished dancing with Mona, take me for a spin around the room."

David laughingly saluted Thelma. "Yes, Viscountess. Your wish is mine to command."

Wallis Simpson walked up to the group. "David, darling, ask me to dance."

Ignoring Simpson, David smiled and took

Mona's hand, leading her onto the ballroom floor. "See what I mean. Bossy women plague my life."

"I think you like the attention, Sir."

He grinned. "You've caught me and call me David please. I get enough of *Your Royal Highness* and *Sir* at Buckingham Place and Fort Belvedere."

The band played a popular show tune while the guests encircled the couple to watch them dance.

As they danced a foxtrot, Mona realized the Prince was a superb dancer, which made her look good. She prayed she wouldn't stumble or step on the man's feet.

Others joined them on the dance floor after several minutes, giving Mona a chance to ask questions. "Are you and Robert really cousins?"

"Perhaps first cousins about six hundred years ago. Why do you ask?" David looked askance at Mona. "You're not wanting to be a royal, are you? Take it from someone who knows. Robert's family being decommissioned, so to speak, from a royal to a noble was the best thing that could have happened to Robert. Believe me. I speak from experience."

"That's an odd word to use. Why were the Farleys *decommissioned*?"

"Robert's father should have married a princess or a royal duchess. He strayed too far from the royal bloodline. Can you believe it? The old man married for the love of a commoner with no money, and my father punished him for it. The King believes in doing one's duty. Marrying for status, heirs, and wealth is the duty for all royals—not love."

"Robert's mother was a commoner?"

"Oh, Robert didn't tell you? My faux pas. Yes, the late Duke of Brynelleth had a bit of bother about the entire affair, but really didn't give a toss. The old gent always did as he pleased. I always admired him for standing up to my father."

"And Robert is repeating his father's folly."

David grinned. "At least, you have money. From what I understand mounds and mounds of money. That is more important than a title nowadays. English aristocrats are an impoverished lot, I'm afraid."

"Would you marry for love?"

"I fall in love several times a year. I'm falling in love with you right now." David pulled Mona closer and pressed his cheek against hers.

"Down, boy. The Viscountess is watching us as is Mrs. Simpson."

David laughed. "Both great lasses. I guess I should behave as there are reporters here."

The dance ended and Mona pulled away. "Thank you, Sir. You have been most gracious. I won't forget."

"Nor I you, Miss Moon." David escorted Mona back to Robert. "I am delivering your bride-to-be safe and sound." The Prince took Mona's hand and kissed it. "We must invite this fabulous couple to Fort Belvedere, Thelma, next weekend. They will add some glamour to that old pile of rocks."

Robert said, "David, may I beg off? I'm doing a tractor demonstration next weekend."

The Prince pouted. "A tractor demonstration? You just get on the thing and ride. What's there to demonstrate? Surely you can put it off?"

Thelma interceded. "David, we must not monopolize this couple's time. Miss Moon has to return to the States soon."

David brightened. "Very well. Another time then?"

Relieved, Robert nodded and silently thanked Thelma.

"Dance with me, David. Make the other ladies wait," Thelma insisted, noticing Wallis Simpon making a beeline for them again.

"Of course, my dear." David led Thelma to the dance floor.

The crowd followed their gaze to the Prince, allowing Robert to ask, "What do you make of David?"

"I think this man doesn't want to be king. Perhaps he will grow into the job though. Many men do."

"It's funny that in the States, men fight each other for the opportunity to be president, but this man, who has inherited the job of ruling, would do anything to be shut of it."

Wanting to change the subject, Mona said, "It was nice of Thelma to invite the Prince. It gives us more wiggle room with the English swells."

"Enough about David. Let's dance, Mona. I feel like kicking up my heels as well." Robert grabbed Mona about the waist and spun her onto the dance floor where they almost bumped into Wallis Simpson dancing with Ribbentrop. "So sorry, old man. Mrs. Simpson. I'm not steady on my pins tonight. War injury."

Ribbentrop nodded graciously and moved away from the couple with Mrs. Simpson in his arms.

Mona said, "You did that on purpose, Robert."

"Maybe. What do you think of them?"

"I think Ribbentrop is encroaching on our circle to spy on us."

"You think he is connected to the death of that young man?"

"Don't know, but I believe Ribbentrop has orders to interfere with us. The murderer of the young man might receive his instructions apart from Ribbentrop."

"What do you think of Wallis Simpson?"

"I think she and Ribbentrop are too cozy with each other to be just good friends, but she has her eye on someone else. Why bother with a German businessman when you can capture the heart of the future king of England?"

"The woman gives me the chills."

Mona reached up and kissed Robert. "Let's forget about the world's problems tonight and enjoy ourselves. This is our engagement party, after all."

"Righto," Robert said, cheerily, sweeping Mona around the room, never realizing that a particular server hired for the evening was carefully observing them.

The server was waiting for an opportunity to strike, but the occasion never arose. Frustrated, the man went through the kitchen ostensibly for a smoking break only never to return. The next morning the butler found the missing man's serving attire thrown into a bin. Thinking the hired server had walked off the job, the butler pocketed the man's wages, hoping to get to a racing track soon.

What no one knew was that the server, whose code name was Le Puma, was rushing to Brynelleth before Robert and Mona arrived the next day.

15

Mona and Robert returned to Brynelleth that Sunday afternoon. Mona could tell the staff was more deferential to her, and associates sent congratulatory telegrams. Mona wondered out loud why the change.

"It's because of this," Violet said, showing Mona the society section of The London Times. It boasted a picture of Mona dancing with the Prince of Wales.

"Oh, goodness," was Mona's response.

"It's a great photograph, but doesn't do the dress justice."

"Read the article to me, please."

Violet shook and then folded the newspaper to the article. *"The Prince of Wales Goes Into Orbit!"* reads Violet. "That's the banner."

"Go on." Mona closed her eyes, anticipating the worst.

"*The Prince of Wales dances with Madeline Mona Moon, American heiress and newly engaged to the Duke of Brynelleth, Robert Farley. Their engagement was announced at the home of Viscountess Thelma Furness. Miss Moon was wearing a silvery chiffon dress embroidered with crystals, elbow length white satin gloves encrusted at the wrist with crystals, and silver pumps, looking out of this world. Miss Moon is the daughter of the late Mathias Milton Moon, a scion of the industrial and mining conglomerate Moon family. The wedding date has not been announced.*"

Violet stopped reading.

"Is that it?"

"That's all."

"Thank goodness there was nothing about my father being disinherited or my uncle being murdered."

"The engagement was also mentioned in the New York Times and the Lexington Leader newspapers."

"How do you know?"

"Because your Aunt Melanie has sent a telegram. Here it is." Violet took the telegram from her pocket and handed it to Mona. "I took it before Mrs. Rymer had a chance to log it in."

"Thank you, Violet. I'll never get used to secretaries going through my mail." Mona opened the telegram with trepidation. Nothing ever good came from her aunt.

YOU PULLED A FAST ONE STOP CONGRATULATIONS I GUESS STOP MELANIE

Mona threw the telegram into the drawing room fireplace and watched it burn, remembering Donovan's warning about hostile forces wanting to remove her as head of Moon Enterprises in favor of her aunt. "Violet, let's get to work. The sooner we head back to Moon Manor, the better."

"I don't think Miss Melanie will try anything since your engagement was announced to His Grace. Right now, she's high in cotton. She'll ride your coattails as far as she can until you make a mistake, and then she'll pounce."

"That's the point. Everyone makes mistakes."

"Even you?" Violet teased.

Mona grinned and playfully elbowed Violet. "Yep, even little old Yankee me."

"It's almost tea time. Shall I ring for it?"

"Please and then let's plan tomorrow. If Mrs. Rymer is still here, ask her to join us."

"Will His Grace want tea?"

"I think he went to meet the new steward and discuss this Saturday's arrangements. He won't be back until dinner. Robert is very anxious that everything goes well for this event. He wants the backing of his tenants to move forward with new improvements."

"I'll check on Mrs. Rymer."

"I'm going to our rooms and have a lie-down for about twenty minutes. I'll need a few moments to myself."

"Our luggage from the weekend is already upstairs. I had one of the footmen take it up."

"Good lass. I'll see you in a few." Mona climbed the stairs and unlocked the door of the late Duchess' bedroom suite. "Oh, my God!" Mona gasped. "Not again!"

The entire room was in shambles. Cushions torn open with their stuffing pulled out. Covers had been ripped from books and tossed on the floor—many of them first editions. The drapes from the windows had been snatched down from the windows. Mona's trunk had been pried opened and her engagement dress had been butchered with a knife. Mona picked the dress off the floor and stared at the large slashes sliced through the dress. Sick at the sight of her dress treated so, Mona grabbed the revolver from her purse and fired a shot out the window before searching the suite for an intruder. He or she still had to be in the suite as the bedroom door had been locked.

The heavy bounding of footsteps sounded up the stairs and down the hallway. Charlie rushed into the suite with Violet close behind. "What's happened?" he barked before taking in the room.

"There's an intruder. He may be in Violet's room," Mona answered, huskily.

Other Pinkertons followed, pushing Violet and Mona into the dark hallway with two Pinkertons guarding them.

Finch yelled up the staircase, "What's wrong? Why all the commotion?"

Mrs. Birdwhistle reached the top of the staircase, wringing her hands when she saw the Pinkertons with their guns drawn surrounding Mona and Violet.

"Ma'am, please return to the ground floor," one of the Pinkertons ordered.

Mrs. Birdwhistle reluctantly descended quietly with nothing to report to the small knot of servants gathering about the flight of stairs stretching their necks to see something— anything.

After several minutes, Charlie and two other Pinkertons came out of the suite shaking their heads. "No one is there."

"Has to be," Mona spat back. "The door was locked and the windows closed."

"I just had the luggage brought up and locked the door myself," Violet added.

"I know," Charlie said. "I saw you lock the door."

Violet looked at her watch. "The room was normal. Nothing amiss. That was a half-hour ago."

"In thirty minutes someone got into my room and ripped it apart—AGAIN." Mona stepped back into the room and picked up her tattered engagement dress again. She clutched it against her heart, fighting back the tears.

Downcast, Violet followed and fingered the

hem of the tattered dress. "Miss Mona, I don't think I can repair this gown."

Mona pressed her hand on Violet's shoulder. "It's alright. We'll get over this. It's just a dress."

"Then why are you weeping?" Violet said, close to tears herself, thinking of all the hard work she had put in sewing the crystals on the dress by hand.

"I wanted to keep it for my daughters. It would have never gone out of style. Someone stole from my future."

The head Pinkerton said, "I'm sorry to interrupt, Miss Moon, but we are going to have to move you and Miss Violet into another bedroom suite."

Mona nodded. "This is what I want. Go find the local locksmith and lean on him to see if he sold a copy of the key to the suite to anyone. Then hire another locksmith from London to put three new locks on the Duchess' bedroom door. Have only the Pinkertons search for hidden panels. If he's not picking the lock, then he's coming through a hidden passage."

"The intruder could have easily entered the room and then locked up again when he left."

"I wouldn't take that chance. Would you with all these people about? Then I want this house searched from top to bottom. Don't use the servants or local men. Just the Pinkertons. Lean on Bertha, too. She might know something."

"Yes, ma'am." The Pinkerton looked exasperated. They had already searched the manor and grounds. They found nothing.

"I want the servants' quarters searched."

Mr. Mott said, "They won't like that."

"I don't care what they like. I need to get to the bottom of this."

"I'm just saying."

Mona said, putting her revolver back in her purse. "I understand, but this time really search. Understand?"

"Yes, Miss Mona."

Mona looked at her watch. "It's tea time. I must go. Violet, come." She and Violet composed themselves as they went down the staircase. At the bottom, a gaggle of servants waited for them. Mona smiled reassuringly. "Mrs. Birdwhistle, is tea ready?" She wanted the servants to return to their duties.

Bertha pushed through the knot of people and

confronted Mona. "Are we going to be murdered in our beds?"

"Do you know something that the rest of us don't?" Mona asked, trying not to show how much she disliked the woman.

"What do you mean?"

"I think you do."

"Nothing but trouble since you came. You're a jinx."

Pulling Bertha's arm, Mrs. Wicket scolded, "Hush, Bertha. That viper's tongue of yours will get thee a comeuppance sooner or later. Come on with me." She pushed the undercook in front of her toward the kitchen.

Mrs. Birdwhistle, wondering if Bertha was correct, was glad for a task to complete. "Yes, Miss Moon. We'll have your tea in a moment. I think Mrs. Rymer is already in the library waiting."

"We would like it now, please."

"Of course. We'll bring it to the library immediately. I'll have Wilbert start a fire. It's chilly this evening," Mrs. Birdwhistle remarked, hoping her tone did not betray her anxiety. Too much upheaval for her taste and the thought that some madman was lurking about Brynelleth caused Mrs. Birdwhistle much distress. She was going to lock her bedroom door until the intruder was apprehended and order the rest of the staff to do so as well.

Something was not right at Brynelleth.

16

Mrs. Rymer stood as Mona and Violet walked into the library. "Thank you for inviting me for tea."

"Mrs. Rymer, didn't you hear the gunshot?" Mona asked.

"Yes, I did."

"And yet I didn't see you in the foyer. Weren't you curious as to the commotion?"

"I was, but heard your men order Mrs. Birdwhistle to stay downstairs. I retreated to the library and had a sit-down. I'm afraid I had a glass of brandy to calm my nerves."

"I think I'll join you." Mona poured herself a brandy while glancing about for the secretary's glass. It sat beside her on a side table. "Violet, do you want something to calm *your* nerves?"

"No, thank you. I think a cup of hot tea will do the trick."

"Very well." Mona took her drink and sat on the couch opposite Mrs. Rymer. "Don't you want to know what happened?"

The social secretary pushed her glasses up with her index finger and nervously smoothed her skirt. "I have a confession to make. I hope you don't hold it against me too badly, but I don't like confusion."

"Confusion?" Violet asked.

"I'm rather humdrum, I'm afraid, and when things get topsy-turvy, I withdraw. Not very heroic, but there it is."

"Mrs. Rymer, my room has been trashed twice, I've been shot at, my beautiful engagement gown has been sliced to ribbons, and you're frightened? All of this is costing me a fortune. I'm beginning to think pumping new life into Brynelleth is a mistake."

"Don't think that, please. What you are doing will have such a positive impact for the village and Brynelleth. We need you. I implore you not to pull your funding."

"And yet, when I call for urgently needed

help, you retreat into the library to hide."

"I realize that I must accept this dressing-down. I behaved badly, but please don't sack me."

"Do you know who is sabotaging me?"

"I don't. I swear."

"I believe someone is using hidden passage-ways in this manor. You were the only person not accounted for because, as you said yourself, you were alone in the library. You could have easily gone into my room from the library and then returned undetected."

"On my word as a Christian woman, I didn't. Please believe me."

Mona studied Mrs. Rymer before saying, "If you are innocent, then you will help me."

"Yes. Yes. Tell me what to do."

"I want you to find the blueprints for this manor."

"It will take some time for me to locate them."

"Where are they?"

"They are in this room. I've only seen them once before His Grace's father hid them."

"Why?"

"I don't know. He never gave me a reason, but I shall search for them."

After a quick knock on the door, Mrs. Birdwhistle had the footman bring in tea, scones, preserves, and little iced cakes.

Mona brightened upon seeing the treats. "Wonderful. Thank you, Mrs. Birdwhistle."

Mrs. Birdwhistle nodded and left the library. She noted that Mrs. Rymer looked very pale.

Mona poured Violet and Mrs. Rymer a cup of tea. "I would like you to start searching after tea. In fact, I think it wise for you to remain here until the blueprints are found."

Mrs. Rymer gulped and replied, "I will need a change of clothes."

"Violet will provide you with a clean frock for tomorrow and a toothbrush. No need for you to rush home and then back again."

Slumping her shoulders, Mrs. Rymer sipped her tea.

Violet looked curiously at Mona. What game was Miss Mona playing?

17

The next morning Robert shook Mona awake. "Why are you and Violet sleeping in my brother's room?"

Mona rubbed her eyes and pushed back platinum hair from her eyes. "Hasn't anyone told you?"

"I got in very late last night. Went straight to bed."

"Shh. Violet's still sleeping." Mona climbed out of bed and slipped on a robe. "Let's talk in your room." They went through the bathroom that connected the Jack and Jill bedrooms.

Robert quietly closed his connecting door. "What's this all about? Are you and Violet all right?"

"Go look in your mother's room."

Robert stormed out with Mona traipsing behind him.

"The door's unlocked," Mona said.

Robert threw open the door and stood just outside the room, looking at the damage. He walked in and picked up Mona's torn dress. "Oh, Mona. I'm so sorry. You and Violet worked months on this dress." He gently draped the dress on a chair and motioned to Mona.

She ran into Robert's arms.

He smoothed her mussed hair, kissing her forehead. "Mona, I think you should go back to Kentucky. Let me finish up here, and I'll join you in the next month or two."

"No, siree. We stick together. I saw how Wallis Simpson licked her chops when she saw you. No way I'm letting you get into her clutches."

Robert chuckled. "Wouldn't do any good. She's not my type. I go for blondes in a big way—not brunettes."

For the first time in fourteen hours, Mona felt good—positive about the coming day. Robert's love for her dispelled any doubts she might have had.

He pulled Mona down on the couch with him

and wrapped his arm around her shoulders. "Let's talk this out. What does your analytical mind say?"

"I think whoever is doing this is travelling through secret panels throughout the manor."

"Mona, I admit this house has secret tunnels and passageways. Alice, my brother, and I used to play in them all the time, but Father had the entrances closed up. Nobody has been in them for over twenty-seven years."

"Well, now you tell me. Don't you think that information would have been useful before-hand?"

"I didn't even think of them. I was very small when Father closed them up, and he forbade us to speak of them."

"Why?"

"I don't know why. Years later he mumbled something about servants spying. I just thought he was being a silly willy."

"Who would know about the passageways?"

"Finch would, but he was forbidden to speak of them as well. I doubt he would have spoken of them to the other servants, and they came into service after the passageways were shut. They wouldn't know about them."

"Do you remember where the entrances are?"

Robert shook his head. "I was five or six, Mona. Alice might. She has a mind like a steel trap."

"What about the architectural plans of the manor?"

"My father had new ones drawn up without any reference to the secret doorways."

"Your father seemed awfully concerned about them. Any guess as to why?"

"Just thought it was one of his eccentricities. As the locals would say—Father was a little bit off his nut."

Frustrated, Mona said, "Robert, this information would have been most beneficial . . ."

Robert cut her off. "You were convinced the new lock had been picked. You said nothing about someone coming through the walls."

"Okay. Okay. Our nerves are frayed. Do you know where your father put the blueprints?"

"They're in my room."

Mona exclaimed, "Your room! Mrs. Rymer searched in the library for hours yesterday looking for them."

"Are you two fighting again?"

Mona and Robert looked up and saw Violet standing in the doorway with Charlie beside her. As soon as he saw that Mona was still in her sleeping attire, he pulled away from the door.

Embarrassed that Violet had caught them quibbling, Robert pushed Mona up from the couch. "Get dressed, my love. I'll meet you for breakfast in twenty." As he rose, he reached underneath and pulled out a garter belt. "So, that's what I've been sitting on."

Mona snatched it away. "Oh, what does it matter." She tossed it over her head, laughing. "Wait for me, Robert. I'll make it ten minutes."

She ran back to her room, but not before stopping in front of Charlie and uttering, "BOO!"

Even Violet had to giggle at Charlie's startled expression. "Miss Mona is in high spirits today."

"Shouldn't a duchess act with more decorum?" Charlie asked Violet.

"Miss Mona is not a duchess yet and if you Pinkertons don't get to the bottom of this mischief, she might not become one."

Charlie grabbed Violet's hand. "Don't eat with

Miss Mona today. Have breakfast with me in the servants' dining room."

"Why?"

"I enjoy your company. Don't you enjoy mine?"

Violet blushed and pulled her hand away. "Maybe."

"So?"

"I'll meet you in the servants' wing in about ten minutes. Right now I have to help Miss Mona."

"She can dress herself."

Violet gave Charlie an odd look. "Besides my mother, Mona means everything to me."

"I'm sorry. I didn't mean to be curt." He gave Violet an endearing smile. "Forgive me."

"I'll be down in a few minutes."

"I go on duty within the hour, so don't tarry too long."

Violet nodded and left to help Mona. Something about this exchange with Charlie bothered her, but she couldn't put her finger on it.

Perhaps it would come to her later.

18

"What did you find?" Mona asked Mr. Mott, the head Pinkerton.

"We found this at Mrs. Rymer's house." He handed Mona several photographs of Mrs. Rymer with Mr. Nowak frolicking on a beach. Mrs. Rymer looked happy and Mr. Nowak gazed fondly at her.

Mona flipped the picture over. On the back written in pencil was *June 1934 Brighton Beach.* "I wonder who took the picture."

"I would say it's one of those holiday pictures. Freelance photographers take pictures of people on the beach and then they are asked to pay if they want a copy."

"Yes, I see a watermark on the photograph."

"Want me to check the company out?"

"No need."

He handed over a two letters on blue paper. "These seem to be love letters between the two of them."

Mona opened a letter. "It's in Polish. I'll hang on to these as well." She put the packet of letters into a large envelope. "Will she know that you searched her home?"

"We left it neat as a pin."

"Good, she's going home after breakfast."

"Mrs. Rymer will never know we were there." Mr. Mott reached for the photograph.

"I want to keep this for now. Thank you." Mona put the photograph in an envelope as well. "What did you find in the servants' quarters?"

The Pinkerton placed several articles on the desk.

Mona picked up some French girlie postcards and looked at the ladies in various states of undress. "Who likes these?"

"Wilbert, the First Footman."

Mona chuckled. "So Wilbert likes the ladies. I was thinking it was the other way around."

"Miss?"

"Nothing. Put them back. I'm not interested

in this. Let's see what else you have." Mona picked up several pamphlets promoting the British Union of Fascists. "This is interesting. Whose room?"

"Bertha's."

"This explains her hostility. I'll keep these as well."

"Very good."

"Thank you for such diligence."

"Miss Moon, we can't keep up this pace. We don't have enough men to do all the things that are needed to keep you and His Grace safe. We still have no clue as to who shot at you or rummaged through your rooms."

"I should have brought more men with me," Mona admitted. "It's too late to bring in rein-forcements from home since we'll be leaving in several weeks. This is on me, Mr. Mott."

"We can hire locally."

"We do need more men to help with the fete this weekend, but frankly, I don't trust anyone from England. This country is teetering toward pro-Nazism. Even the Prince of Wales admires Hitler. My belief in democracy and my dislike of fascism are well known."

"You are considered left-wing by many."

"And right-wing by others, but I have always considered myself simply a follower of Christ, and I want to help others during this Depression. I know what it means to be broke and out of work. What people believe is determined from their own prejudices. I can't help their perceptions of me. I have a chance to do good with the money my uncle left me, and I intend to do the best I can. I may not always succeed, but I'm going to give it a shot."

"People say you upset the natural order of things."

Mona laughed. "You mean because I believe women should have control over their own lives and finances without any interference by men?"

"Among other ideas of yours."

"I guess I am a radical then. A free thinker. Blame my father for teaching me to reason on my own. Here's one thing you can bet on. I will not be bullied into selling copper to the Nazis. I don't like their message or their tactics. There's something very iffy about them."

"It is well known that His Grace mistrusts the Germans and blames them for his brother's death. This trouble might not have anything to do with you, but with His Grace's feelings. He has made his views very public."

Mona tapped the desk, impatiently. "What is it you are trying to say, Mr. Mott?"

"We should go home now. I don't have enough men. I fear this trip is going to end in failure."

"You mean that His Grace or I will be killed."

"I don't want to see one of my men killed as well."

"I trust you don't speak of this to the other men."

Seeing Mr. Mott's back stiffen, Mona knew she had struck a discordant note. "Is there anything else?"

"No, Miss."

"Very well, then. Thank you. Can you ask Finch to come in, please?"

Mr. Mott nodded and left gladly. A plate of eggs, sausage, fried tomatoes, and baked beans awaited him. He had taken a liking to heavy English breakfasts, and Mrs. Wicket always saw to it that had second helpings. It never occurred to Mr. Mott that he was overeating as a way to deal with his frustrations, but the buttons on his pants' waistbands were in need of moving over.

Mona perused the BUF pamphlets until Finch entered the library. He blanched when he saw them in her hand.

"You wish to speak with me, Miss?"

"Have a seat, Finch."

"I prefer to stand, Miss."

"As you wish." Mona cocked her head to one side studying the elderly man. "Have you always worked here, Finch?"

"I was born on the estate. My parents worked for His Grace's grandparents."

"Then you know where all the bodies are buried."

Finch's eyes widened. "Excuse me, Miss?"

"We are searching for the blueprints that show the hidden tunnels and passageways in the manor. Do you know where they are?"

"His Grace has a copy in his room."

"The plans he has were redone omitting the secret passageways. Where are the originals? If anyone knows their whereabouts, it would be you."

Finch stared at the floor.

"Finch?"

"I can't say, Miss."

"Can't or won't?"

"Please, Miss. Don't ask anymore. Some things are best left alone."

"We think someone has reopened the passageways and that's where the intruder is hiding."

Finch trembled a bit before he looked at Mona. "That's impossible. The entry ways were all sealed and cannot be reopened without me knowing about it."

"His Grace may be the target of someone's rage. Surely the Farley family has treated you well all these years. You have had a home here for over sixty years. Will you pay them back by letting Robert, the only living Farley scion, be hurt or killed?"

"I was sworn to secrecy."

"By whom and why?"

Finch strode over to the library door and quickly swung it open. Satisfied that no one was eavesdropping, Finch closed the door and made his way back to Mona. "May I sit, Miss? My legs seem a bit unsteady."

Mona waited for the gentleman to sit and collect his thoughts.

"If I tell the secret, Miss, you must never reveal it to His Grace."

"That serious?"

"I think so." Finch waited for Mona to reply.

"I promise if I think keeping your secret will bring no harm to His Grace."

Finch hesitated before saying, "I will trust you, Miss Moon, because I think you really love His Grace."

"I do, Finch, and you can take that to the bank."

Finch gave a ghost of a smile as he knew Mona loved speaking in idioms. "The Duke burned all the blueprints that showed the secret panels and doorways after they were securely fastened shut. The servants were forbidden to speak of them even amongst themselves on pain of being discharged without references."

"Why?"

"It was because of His Grace's mother."

"The late Duchess?"

Finch nodded. "The Duke and the Duchess were going through a bad patch when the old

master got it into his head that his wife was . . ."
Finch hesitated, "seeing someone."

"This was around the time when His Grace was five?"

"Yes, Miss."

"And the old Duke believed that Robert's mother was having her lover slip through the hidden passageways for a midnight tryst?"

"Yes, Miss, especially in her bedroom."

"Any proof of his suspicions?"

"I never saw any indication. I thought he was off his head. Excuse me for being so coarse. I hate to speak ill of the dead, but my old master was a sweet but odd man. Once he got an idea into his head, he couldn't be disabused of it."

"Do you have any idea who His Grace's father thought was sporting his wife?"

"The horse master. He was fired and the horses were sold."

"That explains why the stable is in such shambles."

"Yes, Miss."

"What happened between Robert's parents?"

"They were estranged for almost a year, barely speaking to one another, but then things changed between them and the Duchess became pregnant."

Startled, Mona drew back in her chair. "And?"

"Her Grace became seriously depressed when she lost the baby. With her husband's support, she rallied, and they became a devoted couple. They were lovely. I was proud to serve them. When the Duchess died, my master grew so despondent that he let things go. Didn't have an interest in anything after she passed." Finch looked pleadingly at Mona. "You won't tell Robert—I mean His Grace?"

"No, I won't. I don't think he needs to know of this discord with his parents. Like you said, some things should be left alone."

Finch stood. "May I attend to my duties now, Miss?"

"Is there anything else?"

"No, Miss."

"Why do I get the feeling I will only ferret out information from you on a need-to-know basis?"

Finch said nothing. The silence hung in the room between them.

Giving in, Mona said, "Very well. You are dismissed."

Finch gave a nod of his head and retreated to the butler's pantry where he had been polishing the silver.

As soon as Finch left the room, Mona rang up Lady Alice's telephone. After several rings, the housekeeper answered the telephone and put the receiver on the side table while she sought out Lady Alice. "Hello? Hello? Alice, is that you finally? You must have been in the garden. Look, I need backup. I want you and Ogden to come stay with us at Brynelleth earlier than planned. No, don't wait until the weekend. Come now. I need help. Yes. Yes. I'll expect you on the evening train. Wait a minute, Alice. Have Ogden bring one of his professor friends who reads Polish. Yes. That's what I said. Reads Polish. See you tonight. Thank you. Bye."

Mona hung up the receiver. Maybe now she could get the answers she needed. There was a code of silence within the village and Brynelleth which she needed to break through. The thought of returning home with secrets and an unknown assassin hanging over their heads was unfathomable.

No way was Mona going to take that darkness back to Moon Manor.

19

Mona opened the door to the local printing shop, which smelled pleasantly of ink and grease. A bell on the door rang.

A man came out from the back room to the front counter, wiping his hands with a rag. "Good afternoon, Miss Moon. I didn't expect you to call in on my shop so soon. Getting ready to send out wedding invitations?"

"Good afternoon, Mr. Prussett. Do you have a moment?"

"Why of course."

Mona pulled a fragment of the threatening letter she had received. "Can you tell me something about this type of print?"

Mr. Prussett took the fragment and laughed when he saw. "I printed this myself."

"You did?"

"This is the same type we use for the Church of England Church's bulletins. I use it for the Sunday programs every week. The church is close to a thousand years old, and the minister requested that we use a type that resembled calligraphy the monks might have used at the time."

"There was a monastery nearby?"

"Yes, but old King Henry tore it down when he pulled away from the Roman church."

"So this is cut and pasted from the church bulletins?"

Mr. Prussett scratched his ear. "Yes, Miss Moon. It would appear so."

"How can you be so sure?"

The printer pointed to the letter e. "See this little squiggle on the bottom of the 'e'?"

"Yes."

"I carved that block myself, so I could always identify my work."

"I see. How many people do you think have access to these bulletins?"

"About half the village. The rest are Catholics, Calvinists, or not interested in religion. Now I'm not saying those people don't believe in God.

They just don't like church. The non-attendees, I mean." Mr. Prussett looked panicky as he was afraid he had offended Mona since he had not seen her at services—nor the current Duke for that matter.

"Is there a particular person who picks up the bulletins or do you deliver?"

"Oh, Mrs. Rymer picks them up every Friday, rain or shine. She takes them to the church for me. Saves me a trip. She's such a nice person."

"Oh. Mrs. Rymer you say."

"Is this the print style you want for your wedding invitations?" Mr. Prussett looked excitedly at Mona, desperately wanting the job. It would raise his status in the village to get the commission rather than a printer from London. "We have a nice rag paper that would do nicely."

Mona looked at her watch. "Mr. Prussett, I must hurry. I'm meeting friends at the train station."

"I also have a nice ivory linen paper. Very elegant for a wedding."

Mona reached for the letter fragment and tucked it back into her purse. "Thank you, Mr. Prussett, I'll be in touch." She left the printing shop, thinking she was getting close to finding those responsible for the death of the American agent and the sabotage at Brynelleth.

She couldn't help but think of Benjamin Franklin's saying—*three people can keep a secret if two of them are dead.* Mona felt that more than one person was involved in a plot against her and Brynelleth. She wondered if they would turn on each other.

20

Mona rushed onto the train platform to greet Lady Alice Nithercott and her husband, Ogden. "Alice! Ogden! Over here."

Alice looked up from paying a porter to retrieve their trunks. "Mona. Oh, Mona. So good to see you." She gave Mona a big hug.

Amused, Mona said, "We just saw each other last weekend."

"Wasn't that dreadful?" Alice quipped. "All those fascists under one roof, not to mention that Wallis Simpson woman—where do I start?"

Mona intertwined her arm around Alice's as they strolled to the parking lot. "Wasn't my engagement party fun at all?"

Laughing, Alice said, "It was the only highlight of the weekend. Now tell me. What is so

183

important that you needed us to come early for this weekend's fete and bring a linguist with us?"

Mona stopped and turned, spying Ogden following, smoking his pipe. Beside him walked a man of medium height with fair unruly hair and light blue eyes topped by eyebrows that arched into a peak. His shoulders were wide, his waist trim, and his lips ruddy. In other words, he looked like a healthy, stout fellow with strong Viking roots. He looked very young, too young to be a full professor.

He stared back at Mona.

"Let me introduce you," Alice said, when Ogden and the stranger caught up with them. "Mona, this is Sidney Ainsworth. Mr. Ainsworth, this is Mona Moon."

Ainsworth gave a short bow. "So this is the damsel in distress."

Mona shook his hand. "Thank you for coming, Mr. Ainsworth."

"Call me Sidney, please."

"I'm Mona, then. I appreciate all of you coming earlier than planned, but we have been experiencing unsettling events at Brynelleth." Mona pressed Alice's hand. "I need support from my friends, and I need help from a linguist."

"Then I'm your man," Sidney said, proudly, studying Mona's yellow eyes. He had seen such coloring of hair and eyes before, but only in pictures. He hadn't realized that hair could be so free of pigment.

Catching his stare, Mona gazed back. Sidney blushed and glanced down at his feet, grinning sheepishly.

Ogden slapped him on the back. "I can vouch for him, Mona. I've never met anyone better than Sidney with languages or code breaking."

"Tell us what is happening," Alice insisted.

Mona looked about the train station. "I will, but in the car. Please follow me."

Two Pinkertons appeared out of nowhere and took the trunks from the porters. Sidney seemed a bit unnerved by their sudden appearance, but said nothing—only giving Ogden an odd glance.

Ogden made a face, shrugging. "You get used to it. Mona's life is a bit unconventional."

Mona and Alice got into the front seat while the men sat in back. Everyone listened expectantly to Mona, who gave a quick rundown of what had been happening at Brynelleth, leaving out the death of the American agent.

"It sounds like disgruntled employees," Sidney responded.

"It's more than that. I've been sent death threats and shot at."

Lady Alice's mouth opened into a surprised O until she remembered to close her mouth.

"Why didn't you say something at the engagement party last weekend?" complained Ogden. "Robert didn't say a word."

"There wasn't enough time or a place in which to speak privately. Ribbentrop and Simpson were always hanging about, not to mention the Viscountess."

"We're here now, Mona. What can we do to help?" Lady Alice asked.

"First of all, can you translate these letters for me?" Mona handed over Mrs. Rymer's letters. "I think they are in Polish."

Sidney opened one of the letters and perused it. Then he opened another and read it.

"I must say this is most unusual reading someone's private correspondence," Ogden remarked, feeling uncomfortable, invading someone's privacy. It was not the gentleman's way.

Lady Alice scolded, "Oh, be quiet, Ogden. Mona's future is at stake. She must use every available means at her disposal to find the culprit who threatens her. You weren't that squeamish with Mona's tactics when I was kidnapped."

Ogden coughed and looked away.

Sidney looked up. "These letters are not in Polish. They are in German—a dialect referred to as Low Franconian, spoken along the Lower Rhine. It is more similar to Dutch than to High German. Most Germans don't speak it anymore."

"What type of person would use this type of German?" Mona asked.

"Definitely someone who lived near the Netherlands. Maybe a German who immigrated there. Would have to be middle-aged or older. I don't think young people speak it anymore."

"What would be the person's education level?"

"Could be a simple laborer or a school teacher. This is an informal way of speaking on the streets. However, this is inexpensive blue stationery. I don't think a person of means would have used this particular variety." Sidney sniffed the letters. "Not scented."

"This is the second packet of letters I've come across. My companion, Violet, saw letters being passed from Wallis Simpson to a German, but she said the letters were written on ivory linen with an embossed crest," Mona mused.

"What connection do those letters have with these letters?" asked Sidney.

"Probably nothing," Mona admitted. "Just thinking out loud."

"And who is Wallis Simpson?" Sidney asked, looking at Ogden, who shrugged back.

Alice asked, "How is it signed?"

"Can't make out the signature."

"Do you think a man or a woman wrote them?"

"It looks like a man's scrawl, but I'm not a handwriting expert."

Alice asked, "Can you translate them, Sid?"

"I will do my best if given a quiet room and time."

Mona demanded, "You must keep those letters a secret. Don't let the servants know you have them."

Sidney grinned, exhibiting a small chip on his left incisor. "I must say this cloak and dagger is intriguing."

The Pinkertons, sitting in another car, honked their horn, giving two short blasts.

Mona started her car. "Looks like my body-guards are impatient for their lunch."

Sidney looked out the rear window and waved at the irritated men in the vehicle behind them. He put the letters in his pockets. "Ogden is good with languages, too. We should have something for you by dinner."

"I want my luncheon first, old boy." Thrusting his head between Mona and Alice, Ogden asked of his wife. "What will you be doing, Luv, while I'm working with Sid?"

Mona cut in. "I have something special planned for Lady Alice. She'll be with me."

"That does nothing to alleviate my anxiety about my wife's safety, Mona," Ogden said.

"Now, Ogden, Mona has saved my life twice now. She needs our help, and we're going to help her. Is that understood?"

"Yes, Alice, quite so." Chastised, Ogden leaned back in the car seat, flipped his hat over his eyes, and settled in for the ride to Brynelleth.

"That seems like an excellent idea, Ogden," Sidney said, so he too leaned back into his seat.

Before long both men were slightly snoring.

Mona and Alice glanced in the rearview mirror and shook their heads.

"I swear bombs could be going off and Ogden would take a snooze," Alice complained.

"Steady on, lass," Mona teased. "There'll be time enough for drama later."

Alice snorted and rolled down her window for fresh air.

The car was quiet for once. Mona took the opportunity to speak seriously with her great friend. "Alice."

"Yes?"

Mona kept her eyes peeled on the road. "If something happens to me, will you look after Robert? Make sure he doesn't start drinking again."

"Nothing is going to happen to you. Don't say things like that."

"But if something does happen."

"Mona, you're making me angry. Nothing is going to happen to you. You've been in tight spots before. We'll sort this mess out. You'll see."

Mona pressed her lips tightly together in dismay. There was no use pressing the issue. If someone had orders to kill her, there was nothing she could do about it.

It would happen sooner or later. Good thing Mona had already made out her will.

21

The men had retired to Sidney's room where a desk had been placed while Mona and Alice took a tour of Brynelleth.

"It's been years since I've been here," Alice said, pushing back a raven wisp of hair into place. "I think the last time was . . . I don't know . . . before I went to Mesopotamia with Father. I know it was after I broke my engagement to Robert. It was run down even then." She looked around, teasing, "I see you got the cobwebs down. No really, everything looks shipshape, Mona. Slowly but surely, Brynelleth is coming back to its former glory."

"We're still working on the roof. The kitchen has been modernized, but no central heating or enough bathrooms. I hate to tell you what the servants have to go through to take a decent bath."

"It's that way in all these old country homes. Don't beat yourself up over it. Things will improve over time. Just think of it, Mona, twenty years ago these houses didn't have any electricity, indoor plumbing, or telephones."

Mona said, "I remember those days. Light by smelly kerosene lamps. The soot left by coal heat. Keeping food from spoiling using ice boxes or root cellars. Thank goodness we can keep things cleaner and safer now. Let's go upstairs. I want to show you something."

"I'm right behind you."

Both women went up the stairs chitchatting until they reached the second floor.

"I need for you to see something," Mona said.

"All right."

"Let's go to the Duchess' bedroom."

"What about?" Alice followed Mona down the long hallway to the bedroom, passing Mr. Mott who was guarding the upstairs.

Alice peeked inside the open doorway and witnessed Violet snipping the crystals off Mona's engagement dress. "Violet, what are you doing?

Stop!" Alice rushed in and grabbed the gown from her.

"She's doing as I asked," Mona said. "Hold the dress up, Alice. To the light, dear."

Bewildered, Alice held up the dress to the windows exposing the slashes. "Who carried out this abomination?" Alice cried, angrily. "Who did this, Mona?" She handed the dress back to Violet and then did a turn about the room taking in the destruction. "It's one thing to hear about the sabotage and another to see it first-hand." She flung herself on the couch next to Violet, who was fiddling with the dress. "Did they destroy all your clothes?"

"Most of their fury was taken out on this dress. Violet has salvaged what she could."

Alice patted Violet's knee. "I'm so sorry, my dear, but were your things bothered as well?"

"No, just Miss Mona's."

"Between the time we arrived from our visit with Viscountess Furness and went upstairs to unpack, someone had entered this room and threw a hissy fit. It was no more than half an hour."

"I would say it was more than a hissy fit, Mona. It was a warning. My first thought would be a servant who holds a grudge."

"The Pinkertons brought up the trunks and Violet locked the bedroom door." Mona shook her head. "We questioned everyone. No servant was on the second floor during this time period. I think the culprit got through the passageways behind the walls."

"They've been shut for years. Robert's father had them sealed."

"Do you know why?"

"No, I was about Robert's age. We were very young—five or six. I can remember I was cross with his father for doing so because he locked up one of my favorite dollies and wouldn't retrieve it."

"Why were you here so often?"

"Father was away most of the time on a campaign, so Mother would call on the Duchess. They would trade visits at least several times a week for tea and luncheon. I think both women were very lonely and their companionship eased that burden."

"So you and Robert would play in the passageways?"

"Hide and seek. Pirates finding lost treasure. Playing tricks on the servants. That sort of thing. We also played in the stables and the garden. It was a wonderful childhood."

"Can you remember how to get inside the passageways?"

"Not really. It was always Robert's brother who opened the doorways."

"Can you try, Alice?"

"Yes, of course. It should be a matter of logic. In my house entrances to secret rooms and passageways were around stairs, fireplaces, or in libraries."

"Why all the need for secret rooms and passageways?" Violet asked.

"For several reasons," Lady Alice explained. "In case of an emergency was one. One never knew when the king would send his men to throw the master of this keep into the Tower of London, so the master would need an avenue of escape to France or until the king cooled down. Another favorite was romantic couples needing a way to visit each other's rooms without the attention of their spouses or servants. Remember, married noble couples rarely slept together in the same bed."

"Hanky panky."

"Exactly, Violet." Lady Alice stood and studied the room. "We can exclude the outside walls and the one adjoining the hallway, so it must be this wall with the fireplace."

"I've tried the fireplace, but I can't find an entrance," Mona said.

"Oh, ye of little faith," Alice commented, going over to the white marbled fireplace and pulling the screen aside. She felt along the wall butting up against the fireplace, fiddled with the knobs on the andirons, ran her fingers across and underneath the mantel, pressed the eyes on the carved angels buttressing the heavy mantel, and stepped on the hearth bricks. Nothing.

Alice gave the fireplace another study.

Mona and Violet pulled up chairs to watch Alice as the guard peeked inside the room to observe as well.

Alice pressed on the bricks inside the firebox until her hands were filthy with soot. Wiping her forehead, Alice dirtied her face as well.

Mona tried to offer her a handkerchief, but Alice refused.

"Don't interrupt. I'm on the hunt." Alice reached up inside the fireplace and felt along the damper and the chimney. "I found the switch!" she cried, triumphantly, stepping back as a panel opened.

Mr. Mott rushed inside and shoved Alice aside while peering into a black hole.

"My good man. You've forgotten yourself," Alice complained.

"Get some flashlights. We're going in," Mona said to Mr. Mott.

As he went into the hallway and yelled down the stairwell requesting flashlights, Mona picked up a poker. "Tell them you want torches," she said to the Pinkerton as she, Violet, and Alice stepped inside the secret hallway. "They don't call them flashlights."

"Look at this," Alice said, pointing to the floor. Footprints were clearly visible in the dust. "You were right, Mona. Someone was using this to get back and forth within the manor."

Wilbert ran up the stairs. "Here are some torches, sir."

Mr. Mott said, "I'm gonna lock this bedroom door behind me. You run and get some of my compadres. I want this hallway guarded until I get back."

"Yes, sir."

The Pinkerton went back inside the bedroom, "Ladies, I must request that you wait downstairs."

"No way," Mona insisted, holding up her fire-place poker. "We're going with you."

Alice and Violet nodded in concurrence, each grabbing one of the torches.

Mr. Mott reluctantly locked the bedroom door. "You're the boss, but stay behind me," the Pinkerton groused, pulling out his gun and stepping into the passageway.

Mona was close behind him, excited to give chase. Lady Alice and Violet brought up the rear. Violet sneezed and then sneezed again.

"Violet!" Mona chastised.

"I'm sorry, Miss Mona, but it is all this dust," Violet whispered, apologizing.

"Hush!" scolded the Pinkerton. "The villain may still be within these walls."

With those sobering words, the three ladies buttoned their lips and looked for clues along the way. After several minutes, they came to a landing where there was a bedroll, a cache of canned food, fake mustaches and eyebrows, various outfits including a parson's collar, wigs, and a slop jar for human waste.

Mona softly groaned. She had been right about the intruder. This explained the sabotage, the sightings of ghostly apparitions, and the missing tools.

"Lady Alice, here is a children's tea set," Violet said, picking up a porcelain doll placed at a small table with two chairs.

"That's Penny, my dolly," Lady Alice said excitedly. She took the doll from Violet and cradled it. "After all these years, I found you, sweet girl." Tears formed in her eyes. "This is where Robert and I must have had tea parties. I think I remember Finch being a footman then and bringing us iced cakes and milk when we played here on rainy days. I wonder why the old Duke wouldn't get me my doll."

"She looks in good shape, Lady Alice. I could make new clothes for her, if you like," Violet offered.

"Look, Miss Mona," Mr. Mott said, pointing to a high powered rifle with a telescopic sight standing in a corner. He picked it up and opened the chamber. "It's got live ammunition in it."

"Take it with us," Mona said, picking up a box

of ammunition and putting it in her pocket. "Let's move on."

The only way forward was down a steep, narrow staircase which ended at a blocked wall.

"Alice?" Mona requested.

Alice moved past the Pinkerton and searched the wall for a switch or lever. "Oh, here it is!" She pulled on a lever and a panel opened slightly. She pushed, but couldn't get the section to swing open.

"Let me try," the Pinkerton said. Grunting, he pushed the panel open with his shoulder allowing all four of them to pass through into the library.

"Well, I'll be," Violet said, looking back and forth from the library to the secret route. "It's a bookshelf. No wonder it was so heavy. It's loaded with books."

Mona said to the Pinkerton, "Close it up and don't let the servants know. I want this kept quiet."

Hearing footsteps, Mona, Lady Alice, Violet, and Mr. Mott stepped back into the opening and pulled the door closed. Quietly, they went back up the stairs to the landing and then out into the bedroom. The four brushed dust and cobwebs from their attire before unlocking the door.

Two other Pinkertons and Wilbert, waiting in the hallway, looked expectantly at them. "What did you find?" one of the guards asked.

"Nothing. We thought we had found the secret tunnels, but it turned out to be a sealed closet," Mona said.

"A sealed closet?" Wilbert asked in surprise. "Why would anyone seal up a closet?"

"It looked to me like a failed attempt at a bathroom. Lots of rat droppings. We're going to our rooms now. No need to be here. Go about your duties," Mona said to the three men. She started to say something else but the dinner gong rang. Wilbert scurried downstairs while the two Pinkertons gave Mr. Mott a curious look before taking their leave.

Once they had gone, Mr. Mott turned to Mona. "What are your orders concerning this?"

"Stick with the abandoned bathroom story."

"No one is going to buy that for a moment."

"But they can't be sure. I need time to come up with a plan. Just bear with me."

"It's your money, Miss."

"You better get your dinner now."

Mona, Violet, Lady Alice, and Mr. Mott turned when they heard clumping up the stairwell.

"What's all this?" Robert said, surprised at seeing the four standing in a little knot.

"Nothing, dear," Mona said, reaching up and kissing Robert on the cheek, which he returned.

"Alice, so nice of you to volunteer for this weekend. I'm hoping it's going to be smashing." Robert gave her a quick peck as well.

"After the help you gave me with Father's estate, of course, I would be here. I'm looking forward to the tractor demonstration."

"Where's Ogden?" Robert asked, looking about the hallway. He got a blank stare from everyone. "Is something wrong?"

"Nothing, dear." Mona gave a slight nod of her head, giving Mr. Mott permission to leave. She turned her attention to Robert. "Did you hear the dinner gong?"

"I did."

"When you use the bathroom, can you leave the door ajar?"

"What?"

"Just slightly. All the Pinkertons are downstairs. I would feel safer if you could hear me if I called."

"You and Violet dress first. I'll leave the door open just a tad. Knock on it when you're finished. I'll finish up and meet you both downstairs."

"You won't peek, will you, Your Grace?" Violet asked, looking up at him.

"I stopped peeping at little girls when I was eight. Besides, you don't have anything I haven't seen before, but I give my word as a gentleman not to peek."

"That doesn't reassure me," Violet huffed. "I know how English gentlemen can be."

Robert's eyes narrowed, wondering where Violet was going with this accusation. He had given her no cause not to trust him. "I don't know how you can suspect me of such bad behavior, Violet."

Mona intervened, knowing that Violet was blowing off nervous steam. "Robert, Violet is joking."

"Are you? You had me going. I have a mind to spank you, young lady. Not very sporting, I must say."

Laughing, Violet headed to her room to change for dinner.

Lady Alice announced, "If you will both excuse me, I should find Ogden. He must be around here somewhere." She trotted off to her room, thinking she would collect Ogden from Sidney's room once Robert had retired. She wasn't sure what Mona had revealed to him and didn't want to upset the apple cart.

Once they were alone in the hallway, Robert pulled Mona into his room. Picking her up, he threw her on the bed, flopping beside her.

"Robert, Violet will hear," she said, listening to water running in the bathroom.

"Just give me five minutes, woman," Robert insisted. "I haven't had you in my arms for weeks and I'm burning with a fever."

"That's a line from a Mae West movie."

"Is it? Too bad." He kissed Mona passionately until she pushed him away. "What is it now?" he asked, annoyed.

"Do you think you're the only one whose blood boils? Have some pity on me, Robert." Sexually frustrated as well, Mona rose and stumbled to the door. "We can't indulge ourselves at the moment. Village gossip and all that. See you at dinner, my love."

Robert blew Mona a kiss as she went out the door to her own room. Whistling, he pulled off his boots, happy in the knowledge he could still make Mona's knees buckle with his kiss. It boded well for a happy marriage. He couldn't wait to put that gold band on her finger, get on with his life, and leave this tumbling pile of rocks called Brynelleth behind.

22

Everyone worked feverishly for the next several days getting Brynelleth ready for Saturday's party. The entire village was invited.

The fields were mowed, fences repaired, the garden pruned and preened, the driveway refreshed with new pea gravel and the weeds removed, and Mr. Nowak fixed the fountain so that the water flowed clear and free. Two shiny tractors stood silently near the doorway as Robert did not want anyone to miss seeing them.

Mrs. Birdwhistle made large, showy flower arrangements for Brynelleth while Mrs. Wicket baked tiny chocolate cakes, cinnamon buns, apple fritters, jam tarts, raspberry jelly loaves until there was no more sugar available from the village store. In addition, she had help from the local women making single pork pies, pot pies, cucumber sandwiches, and hard-boiled eggs.

A large tent was set up on the lawn west of Brynelleth and every available table and chair was cheerfully confiscated for service. Robert had the hotel pub set up a temporary bar inside the tent where adult guests would be given three free ales plus all the soda pop, tea, or lemonade they wanted when they showed their ticket which they would receive when they came through the estate's gates. No hard liquor would be allowed as Robert needed the local men sober for the demonstrations.

Violet found an odd closet packed with old sheets which she confiscated and used as table clothes for the tables. She and Sidney took charge of the tent and happily bantered with each other as they decorated the tables and put up colorful streamers. Sidney regaled Violet with stories about being a professor at Cambridge, making her laugh. She regarded Sidney as a bright spark during this dreary trip and enjoyed his relaxed personality.

In addition to the musicians whom Robert had hired, Mrs. Rymer procured a juggler, an animal balloon maker, and a fortune teller from London with instructions to give only happy fortunes.

At ten in the morning, Mona, Robert, Lady Alice, Ogden, Violet, Sidney, the six Pinkertons, Mrs. Rymer, Mrs. Birdwhistle, Mrs. Wicket, Finch, and the rest of the house staff gaped at the tent.

"It's a mighty fine looking pavilion," Mrs. Wicket announced. She looked at the watch pinned to her shirt. "Won't be long now. We'll be moving the ice out and then the food in about two hours. That will give folks time to look around and settle in. We want them good and hungry."

Mona asked Mrs. Birdwhistle. "Are you ready for tours?"

"Mrs. Rymer and I will be escorting groups of ten through the public rooms and then out through to the west lawn where they can enjoy the refreshments."

Mrs. Wicket looked as though she was about to cry, wiping her eyes with her apron. "I'd never thought I'd see Brynelleth spring back to life as she has. It's a glorious sight for these old eyes."

Mona gave Mrs. Wicket a quick hug as they looked proudly around. Beyond the colorful tent sprang another long mowed field with grazing sheep in the distance. Mrs. Wicket was right. She and Robert, with the help of others, had turned this sow's ear into a silk purse.

Robert looked at his wristwatch. "People will be here in an hour. I think we should all have a cup of tea before they arrive."

Lady Alice seconded. "Sounds like a good idea. I need to catch my breath for a moment."

Suddenly upon hearing a motor car rush toward them on the new pea gravel driveway, everyone turned toward the sound.

"Who the Devil is that?" Robert groused. "The gate is not to be opened until eleven."

The group hurried to the front of the manor to see a red and black Vauxhall Cadet park next to the tractors after coming to a screeching halt. Finch hurried to open the car doors allowing Viscountess Furness, Wallis Simpson, and Herr Ribbentrop to climb out.

"I see that we've arrived in time," gushed the Viscountess. She spread open her arms, making her way toward Robert. "Robert! Robert! Come give me a kiss."

"Bloody hell," Robert murmured under his breath. "What are they doing here? They weren't invited."

Ogden said, "Steady on, Robert. Smile and greet them. Alice and I will take them on."

"So will I," Sidney agreed.

Robert glared at Sidney. "And who are you again?"

"I explained several days ago that Mr. Ainsworth is a friend of Alice and Ogden. I invited him for the weekend, dear. Now be nice, Lord Bob. Let's not cause a scene with the Viscountess. There will be reporters here soon," Mona said, sidling up to Robert and forcing a smile. "Let's just make the best of this."

Robert forced himself to greet the Viscountess, who embraced him tightly, "Thelma, I didn't know you were coming."

"Well, you invited us the night of your engagement, but we had to bully our way in. That young man at the gate wouldn't let us in, so I drove right past him." She whispered, "I didn't invite Ribbentrop. Wallis must have. Please forgive me."

Robert said, hoping to take out the sarcasm in his voice, "It's a lovely surprise."

The Viscountess approached Mona and gave her a tight hug as well. "So happy to see you as well, dear. I hope you don't mind this intrusion. How are you?"

Mona replied, "Fine, thank you."

The Viscountess looked about. "Where is everyone?"

"The event doesn't start until eleven," Robert said, greeting Wallis Simpson and Herr Ribbentrop, who seemed less than impressed with Brynelleth.

Lady Alice stepped forward. "I'm sure Mona and His Grace have a thousand little details to attend. Please let me give you a private tour of Brynelleth and the gardens. Mona has brought Capability Brown's designs back to life again."

Wallis said, "I would kill for a cup of tea or something stronger and somewhere to freshen up."

"I can set up elevenses for you in the library and show you a room where you can powder your nose," Alice said, smiling. "Follow me, Wallis. Viscountess. Herr Ribbentrop, would you care to join us?"

"I don't need to powder my nose, thank you. I think I will examine these tractors. I want to compare English tractors to our newly designed German models."

"I need this car to be relocated," Robert complained. "Sidney will show you around. I have to see to things. Please excuse me."

"Of course, Your Grace," Ribbentrop said, getting back into the Vauxhall Cadet.

Robert leaned over and whispered to Sidney, "Don't let that man out of your sight, Sidney or whoever you are."

"Yes, Your Grace," Sidney replied, making way for the car.

Mona and Violet watched as the new guests disappeared. "This is really going to upset our security protocols with those three," Mona said to Robert.

"Alice and Ogden will keep the ladies busy, but I don't know about Ribbentrop. He's up to something." Robert glanced at Violet.

She shook her head. "I'm already promised to Mrs. Wicket to handle the food in the tent. She's already short-handed as we used the footmen to stand as guards in the public rooms for the tours."

"What are the Pinkertons doing then?"

"Their jobs," Mona replied, patting her forehead with a handkerchief. "Let's not interfere with them. I'll get some of the tenants to help."

"I need them outside to watch the demonstrations. That's what this is all about." Robert took a cigarette out of his silver case. "Don't nag me, Mona. I need a smoke." He lit the cigarette and threw the match on the ground. "Those blasted imbeciles. They've messed up my day."

"Robert, we need to focus. It's getting close to the opening. Let the others handle this for us."

"All right, my American cow. Smile because half of the village is walking up the driveway."

Mona pushed Robert near the front door and called to Mrs. Birdwhistle and Mrs. Rymer. "They're coming. Get ready."

Robert and Mona greeted their guests by the front door and explained that Mrs. Birdwhistle and Mrs. Rymer would take them on a short tour and lead them out to the west lawn for refreshments. Excited that they were going inside Brynelleth, many scuffed their shoes on the pea gravel or the boot scraper to shake off country mud before stepping inside the manor.

After an hour of smiling and nodding politely, Mona asked Mrs. Birdwhistle to take over the official greeting as she needed a break. Robert had already left her side for the tractor demonstration.

Mona followed a tour group inside and ran upstairs to wash her face and put on fresh lipstick.

As Mona closed the door to her room, a man slipped away from the tour group while in the library. It only took a second to hide when everyone's attention was elsewhere. He slid behind the heavy carved library door and waited until the downstairs footman safeguarding the room ran to the bathroom as he figured that was the last group coming through. It was getting on to one o'clock and the fete was to be over at two. Anyway, who would want to steal dusty old books?

The man moved quietly across the floor and pulled a lever hidden behind Gibbon's *Decline and Fall of the Roman Empire*, slipping behind the hidden doorway and closing it behind him.

Feeling he was safe, the man took a torch from his pocket and proceeded to make his way to the landing where he had hidden his Mauser Gewehr 98 rifle equipped with a scope. After retrieving it, he would then make his way to the rooftop where he would kill either Duke Robert Farley or his main target, Mona Moon. He had failed to intimidate Mona Moon, so his new instructions were to take her out. With Mona out of the way, his superiors would be free to strike a deal with her Aunt Melanie, who would be more malleable as head of Moon Enterprises.

His footsteps on the stairway hardly made a sound. Even his breathing was steady and shallow as he thought of how he would mingle with the panicked crowd amidst the ensuing confusion after he had gunned down his quarry. It would be an easy job. *Oh shiza* he thought. His torch was going out. He smacked the torch across his palm and quietly cursed as the bulb flickered and died completely. No matter. He could feel the rest of the way to the landing. Once there he could pull the cord for the light on the south wall. He also kept an extra torch in his backpack stored there as well.

He found the landing and felt along the wall seeking the light cord. Having found it, he grabbed it and gave a tug, flooding the landing with light only to turn to find Mona Moon sitting in a chair pointing a gun at him.

"Le Puma, I expect. We finally meet."

23

Agent McTavish and his assistant stepped out of the shadows with handcuffs. "Sorry, old chap, but I'm afraid you'll be coming with us."

As Le Puma sized up the situation, he turned to escape down the stairs only to run into Mr. Mott and Charlie coming up the stairs with their guns drawn as well.

"We've been waiting for you, Le Puma," Mona said. "We found your rifle days ago, and Mr. McTavish and his men have been hanging about to see if you would turn up for it."

"It was bloody awful, hiding in this room and eating military rations," complained McTavish. "But we were pretty sure you would make your move soon."

"They have been here for three days, taking

turns sleeping in the Duchess' bedroom. No one knew they were here except for His Grace," Mona said. "Before they take you away, I've got to ask—why did you kill that man in the woods? He was so young."

Le Puma maintained a stoic silence.

McTavish asked, "Who was your accomplice? You couldn't have done this on your own. Someone had to provide food while you were hiding here and inform you about Miss Moon's movements."

"I work alone," Le Puma said in an unmistakable American accent. "No one helped me."

The American accent threw Mona for a moment. "You're from the United States?"

"I am."

"Miss Moon, he might be a first generation German immigrant born in the United States with lots of family connections still in Germany. There is a lot of support for *strong men* in your country, Miss Moon," McTavish spoke up.

"As in yours, McTavish," Mona shot back.

Le Puma, ashamed at being caught and failing his assignment, boasted, "America has grown soft and decadent. I work to bring German values to the world."

"The world is a pretty big place," Mona replied.

"We will win. The United States and England are too weak to stop us. You'll see. We'll conquer the world! SIEG HEIL!"

Mona shot up from her seat. "Traitor!" she hissed.

"Steady on, Miss Moon," McTavish suggested.

Composing herself, Mona said, "Keep him here until the tractor demonstration is over, then have your car brought to the front door. Most of the servants will be on the west lawn relaxing and having their tea. They won't see him leave. I need to get back to my duties now."

"Very well, Miss. We can't have you being missed," McTavish agreed.

"I'll leave via the bedroom." She turned to Le Puma. "I hope I never see you again."

Le Puma narrowed his eyes. He radiated a hate that was almost palpable compelling Mona to retreat a step. "There will be others. It won't stop with me."

"'It won't stop with me either. Your people are not getting my copper."

As Mona walked away, he screamed, "IT WON'T STOP WITH ME. OTHERS WILL COME. YOU ARE DEAD, MONA MOON. GIVE US THE COPPER OR YOU ARE DEAD!"

24

Mona met Robert in the pavilion. He was in a jovial mood even though ignoring the little huddle of Thelma Furness, Wallis Simpson, and Joachim Ribbentrop sitting with Lady Alice and Ogden.

Mona asked, "How did things go, dear?"

"Where in the blazes did you hide yourself for the past hour?"

Mona said, "I'll tell you later. I see we still have a few stragglers left."

"Mrs. Birdwhistle is rounding them up and shutting down the house."

Mona rolled her eyes at Wallis and Thelma. "It looks like some people don't get the hint."

"I'll take care of this. Finch! Finch!"

"Yes, Your Grace?"

Robert ordered, "Summon the servants to the tent."

"Everyone, Your Grace?"

"Yes, even the Poles."

Finch hurried off in search of the staff, saying the Duke wanted to speak with them. Bit by Bit, the servants and workmen ventured out into the pavilion where Robert waited.

Once they were all assembled, Robert asked Wilbert and Keelan to fetch everyone a glass of the remaining ale. "I want to thank everyone for their contribution for the past weeks. I know it has been a strain having everyone's routine disturbed, but we achieved much of what Miss Mona and I wanted. I think you will all agree with me that the fete for the village was a success."

Robert held up a list. "We were able to get five tenants to schedule use of the tractors. Hopefully, more men will use the new equipment as time passes. Mona and I have big dreams for Brynelleth, and you are a big part of making those dreams a reality. You will find a token of our appreciation in your next pay packet plus the bonuses we promised."

Twittering, the servants grinned and gleefully

elbowed each other.

"Does that go for us poor roof hoppers, Duke?" Mr. Nowak asked.

"It does indeed when the roof is finished, Mr. Nowak," Mona said. "So you best be hurrying on it if you want your money."

Nowak twisted his lips. "Should have known."

Robert raised his glass of ale. "Here's a toast to Brynelleth—may she continue to provide our sustenance, and let's raise our glasses for the health of our sovereign, King George V."

"Hear. Hear," murmured the small gathering before taking a sip.

"Let's carry the dirty dishes and leftovers into the manor, but leave the rest for tomorrow's cleanup. Everyone has the rest of the day off. Miss Moon and I, along with my guests, will fend for ourselves. Enjoy your evening. Dismissed."

Mrs. Wicket huffed, "I want all the extra food stored in the refrigerators before the kitchen staff runs off to town to see the new Jean Harlow film."

The Viscountess and her two companions wandered over to Robert. "I was hoping you could put us up for the night, but in the light of the fact that you'll have no servants this evening, I'll return home."

"Are you sure?" Robert asked, secretly pleased.

"I have no desire to rough it or prepare my own meals. Who is going to arrange afternoon tea?"

Ribbentrop bowed. "I feel I must concur with the Viscountess. I am shamefully addicted to servants waiting on me. I've become a lazy man. However, it has been a most interesting afternoon, and I thank you for letting us attend."

"My pleasure, sir," Robert said, returning the bow.

Wallis Simpson gave a short salute, saying, "Adios."

"Well, chin chin. Have a safe journey," Robert said. He and Mona walked the three to their Vauxhall Cadet parked near the stables. They put their arms around each other's waists while waving to the retreating car. As soon as they were out of sight, Robert asked Mona, "Well, did we get him?"

"One of them at least."

Mona signaled to the MI5 gent peering out of

a front bedroom window and waved to Mr. Mott to bring their car around. She wanted Le Puma out of the manor as soon as possible. With the staff hurrying to clean up on the west side, this was a perfect opportunity to bring the shackled man to the car.

As the German sniper was driven away by MI5 agents, Mona said to Robert. "We'll empty the rest of the viper nest before we leave."

"Tomorrow. Let's go join Alice and Ogden now. They're waiting for us, and I haven't eaten. I'm going to raid the refrigerator as soon as Mrs. Wicket leaves. I'm starving." Robert picked Mona up and twirled her around. "We did it. Good Golly, we did it, Mona."

Laughing, Mona decided to enjoy this victory over evil as she might not be so lucky later on.

25

Several weeks later, Violet was busy packing Mona's steamer trunks, happy to be going home. Although she had taken a great liking to English fish and chips, she missed her mama's fried catfish, mashed potatoes, and greasy green beans. Violet also missed the rolling green hills of Kentucky—and there was a wedding dress to sew.

As for the engaged couple, most of the work Robert and Mona wanted to accomplish was done. The roof was finished, and the workmen were currently installing three new bathrooms upstairs. Robert was checking the barns for last minute repairs while Mona was downstairs in the library paying the last of the invoices Brynelleth had accrued when she asked Mrs. Rymer to step in.

Mrs. Rymer entered the library with a typed list. "Here is the inventory at last. What a chore, but we got it done."

Without looking up from her checkbook, Mona said, "Hand it to Mr. Dankworth, please."

Mrs. Rymer looked over and was startled to see Mr. Dankworth, one of the estate's solicitors, sitting in the shadows. "I didn't see you, sir."

"Have a seat, Mrs. Rymer. Mr. Dankworth has documents that require your signature."

"Pardon me?"

Mona replied, "First one is a N.D.A."

Mr. Danksorth added, "This is a nondisclosure agreement. Also, we have a confession which we took the liberty of typing up for you."

"A confession?" Mrs. Rymer blinked several times.

Mona looked up from her paperwork. "Are you going to echo everything we say?"

"I'm confused. What's this about, Miss Moon?"

"You are going to leave the village, Mrs. Rymer. Once you are far away and settled elsewhere, you will be sent your monthly stipend for a full year. That will give you some breathing room to find other employment and housing—that is if MI5 lets you."

"MI5? I don't understand. What have I done?"

Mona opened a desk drawer and tossed the ribboned packet of letters with the photograph of Mrs. Rymer with Mr. Nowak. "You shouldn't have kept mementos, especially love letters from a man who is encouraging you to commit fraud and sabotage, Mrs. Rymer. I guess Nowak seduced you. That's what I gathered from the letters."

Stunned, Mrs. Rymer picked up the photograph and turned it over. "You went through my house and my private papers. How dare you!"

"Do you remember Mr. Ainsworth, who stayed with us a couple of weeks ago?"

Mrs. Rymer nodded.

"He's a linguist and translated the letters for me. You and Mr. Nowak have been very naughty."

Mrs. Rymer shot up from her seat and rushed the doorway, but Charlie, who had been standing in the back of the room, slammed the door shut.

"Sit down, Mrs. Rymer. Miss Moon is not

finished," he ordered in a crisp voice.

With her lower lip quivering, Mrs. Rymer sat down uneasily as Mr. Dankworth placed two documents on the desk.

"One thing Mr. Ainsworth told us was that your letters from Mr. Nowak are written in German, not Polish."

"My family came here after the Great War, and we brought German values with us. You forget the current king is from German stock."

"It wasn't German values that caused you to betray your country. We found it interesting how Nowak manipulated you with words of love and the future you two would have together. It was all a lie. Mr. Nowak is an agent for the Third Reich."

"You're lying."

Mona continued, "He's not even Polish. Mr. Nowak is a mercenary hired to work with a man who was sent here to kill me. His words of love are false."

Mrs. Rymer spat out in a brittle voice, "I don't believe you. I've nothing to be ashamed of. Do you think only you and His Grace are entitled to love?"

"Did you know that Nowak means newcomer

in Polish? I'm afraid Mr. Nowak has given you both an alias for a name and the slip, leaving you to hold the bag. He skipped for parts unknown yesterday evening, but my men will track him down."

For the first time, Mrs. Rymer looked worried. "I can explain. He said you were a dangerous radical bent on destroying our way of life here in England—that you were a spy. Marrying Robert Farley was the first step of your grand plan."

Undeterred, Mona continued, "You were the one who hid Le Puma in the manor and brought him food, posed as a ghost dressed in white, and stole tools. Probably on the orders from Mr. Nowak. I could almost forgive you for that, but you were also the one who cut up my engagement dress. You used the secret passageway to go into my room and destroy my gown. That wasn't politics. That was personal."

"Yes, it was me. I hate the sight of you—that gawd awful white hair and those creepy yellow eyes of yours. Robert Farley should marry a genuine English rose and live in Brynelleth, not be traipsing off to some American backwater called Kentucky. I found the original blueprints with all the secret passageways and hidden rooms. It was a lie that the old master destroyed them."

"Finch said the Duke's father burned them."

"The Duke burned only one copy. I found blueprints older than the ones he burned."

"Where are the blueprints?"

"I hid them and won't tell."

Mona could not hide her disgust. "Take the deal, Mrs. Rymer."

"I haven't done anything treasonous. I love my country. I certainly wasn't involved in any murder."

"Why did you think Le Puma was here? He was a member of the Sicherheitsdienst and killed an American agent on the property. You are in big trouble, girlie."

Mrs. Rymer looked surprised. If someone had died, this was the first she had heard of it. "Nobody has been murdered on the estate. You're lying."

"MI5 has your name. They have read the letters. You are in their sights. You will sign your confession with Mr. Dankworth, who will turn it over to MI5. I'm sure they want to make a deal with you. Mr. Nowak might possibly try to get in contact with you again or, at the very least, the German High Command might send someone else to contact you."

"MI5!" Mrs. Rymer quickly felt her forehead as she began to perspire.

"Chief Inspector McTavish is not from Scotland Yard but MI5. He wants to save your scrawny neck for future use." Mona placed the top on her fountain pen and closed the checkbook. Rising from her chair, she said, "Those documents in front of you represent your deal with me. I never want to see you in the village again or for you to have any contact with any member from this house. You will leave Brynelleth never to return. An excuse of a dying aunt will be your cover for leaving. After you sign my papers, you will be met at the gate by an MI5 operative, who will escort you to your house to pack and then take you to London for further investigation. What arrangement you and McTavish make is your own affair. Take the deal, Mrs. Rymer. Save your own skin and take the deal."

As Mona left the room, Mr. Dankworth sniffed haughtily and handed Mrs. Rymer his personal fountain pen and pointed to where she was to sign.

Accepting the inevitable, Mrs. Rymer uncapped the pen and signed her name on both documents. There was no way out of this. Mona Moon had closed every avenue of escape. The only satisfaction Mrs. Rymer had was knowing there was another agent embedded in the Moon household.

Not even Mona Moon had ferreted him out.

26

Mona was ready to go home. She missed Moon Manor, the horses grazing in mist-covered pastures, and the smell of fresh baked bread from her own kitchen. Yes, she was ready to return to her beloved Bluegrass.

Lady Alice, Ogden, and even Mr. Ainsworth showed up at the dock to say goodbye.

"I'll see you at the wedding," Mona said, hugging Alice. "Write to me."

"I shall every week, I promise," Lady Alice said, tearing up.

Robert shook hands with Ogden, saying, "Take care, mate. See you in Kentucky next."

Hating to see his friend leave, Ogden tried to look cheerful. "I will. You as well."

Robert turned to Sidney Ainsworth. "Who are you again?"

Sidney laughed at Robert's confusion, bade him adieu, and walked away, making a beeline for Violet. He thrust a piece of paper into her hand. "That's my address. Will you write to me? I think you are a cracking girl."

Pleased, Violet replied, "I shall be happy to oblige."

Sidney winked and said, "See if you can finagle an invitation to the wedding for me. I'll escort you."

Mona strolled over. "Sidney, your friends are leaving. You'll miss your ride."

Looking over his shoulder, Sidney saw Lady Alice and Ogden hurrying to their car. He doffed his hat for a second and cried out as he ran after them, "Don't forget, Violet. Write to me!"

"It seems you have a new admirer, Violet," Mona commented.

"We're going to be pen pals."

"How nice. Why don't you go on the ship and find our state rooms? I have some unfinished business on the dock."

"Sure. Meet you later."

As soon as Violet was on the ship, Mona motioned to the Pinkertons to follow her to a less crowded section of the dock. Robert followed, bringing up the rear.

"Boys, I'm sorry to say that one of you will not be coming back to the United States with us."

"Why?" asked Mr. Mott. "You can't leave one of us in the lurch like that. It goes against our contract."

Mona held up her hand. "It's not what you think, Mr. Mott. We have what is known as a mole within our midst. A secret operative. A gun for hire."

Mr. Mott argued, "Impossible. The Pinkerton Agency vets everyone. There is no way a mole could have been hired by us."

"But it's true."

"How true?"

"Circumstantial evidence I must admit, but it creates enough doubt that this gentleman must be cut adrift. Charlie won't be coming with us."

Mr. Mott exploded, "CHARLIE! He's one of the best men I have. You must be mistaken."

Mona glared at Charlie. "You made your first mistake by using the word 'tarry'. I read your file. It stated that you have only a high school educa-tion. American boys don't use the word 'tarry', but a lad who attended British schools might."

Charlie gave a rakish grin. "Oops. I must have slipped up when canoodling Violet. I didn't realize she was so perceptive. I had her figured for a dolly bird, but apparently underestimated her."

"I must congratulate you on your American accent, Charlie. You sound like a real Yank."

"High praise, indeed."

"Who do you work for? British Union of Fascists? The Reds from Moscow?"

"Oh, much closer to home. You've angered important men from your own country. They say you stir up trouble with the labor force."

That answer stunned Mona. "I hardly think one of my own countrymen would be working with a German sniper."

"You'd be surprised. Germany's concerns coincide with American ones." Charlie glanced at the Pinkertons surrounding him. Seeing there was no avenue for escape, he asked, "What else gave me away?"

"On the day we went out surveying, you had us stop for our picnic right where the sniper would have an excellent shot at me. Good thing for me the wind was strong that day."

"I guess this has turned into somewhat of a cock-up for me."

Mona asked, "Who killed the American? Was it you or Le Puma?"

"Le Puma, of course. I was with you—remember, but what proof do you have of any of this?"

"I can't prove any of this, but I believe my assumptions to be correct and you have half admitted to it." Mona thumbed at the other five Pinkertons. "These boys are going to put you into a taxi and then guard the entrances to the ship so that you can't double back and get on board before we sail. This is where our journey together ends, Charlie."

Charlie turned his gun over to Mr. Mott. "Be gentle, boys. Don't rough me up. This is a new suit."

Mr. Mott grabbed Charlie's waistcoat and pulled him toward a queue of waiting taxis.

Robert came up to Mona. "Enough, Mona. Enough skullduggery. Let's go home." He crooked his elbow.

Mona put her arm through his and let Robert

escort her up the ship's ramp. Her heart felt lighter. She had survived and won the latest battle, and now she was going back to Moon Manor. "Home," Mona whispered. "Yes, let's go home."

American Isolationism
A popular 1930s social and political philosophy advocating American non-involvement in foreign military conflicts, especially Europe and Asia.

Bolsheviks
Members of the far-left wing of the Russian Social Democratic Party. They separated from the Mensheviks (Those of the Minority) of the Marxist Russian Social Democratic Labor Party, at its Second Party Congress in 1903. Both factions followed the teachings of Karl Marx and his theories of social and economic emancipation through class conflict in The Communist Manifesto and Das Kapital. Vladimir Lenin became

the leader of the Bolsheviks and led them to victory against the White Army (pro-Tzar) in the Russian Civil War in 1917. Lenin most likely ordered the deaths of the Russian Imperial family (the Romanovs) at Yekaterinburg on July 17th, 1918 in order to solidify his power over Russia.

British Union of Fascists

A political party formed by Sir Oswald Mosley, 6th Baronet, in 1932. The party was popular at the beginning of its formation, but as it crept closer to Nazi ideology and anti-semitism, support waned. When the Fascist Defence Force, the paramilitary wing of the BUF, attacked anti-fascist protestors at the Olympia Rally of 1934, many members left the party. The Public Order Act 1936 banned the blackshirt uniforms of the BUF as well as other political groups' uniforms. The organization was banned in 1940 as it was considered a threat to national security as Great Britain fought in WWII. Many members were arrested and detained under the Defence Regulation 18B. Mosley was imprisoned in 1940, released in 1943, and lived abroad in Paris for the remainder of his life.

Charles Lindbergh Jr. (1930-1932)

The infant son of world-renowned aviator Charles Lindbergh and Anne Morrow Lindbergh, was stolen from his crib on the upper floor of the Lindbergh's home on March 1, 1932. At the time it was called the *crime of the century*. The child was found dead by a truck driver on the side of a nearby road. Bruno Hauptmann was arrested and convicted of the kidnapping. He died by the electric chair in 1936. Congress passed the Federal Kidnapping Act, known as the *Little Lindbergh Law*, which made transporting a kidnapping victim across state lines a federal crime. Agatha Christie's *Murder On The Orient Express* was inspired by the Lindbergh kidnapping.

Cottage Loaf Bread

A type of traditional bread that is characterized by a rounded loaf of bread with a smaller topknot of bread attached to the top. Considered a country or rustic bread that originated in England and is similar to a French brioche bread, but has a more irregular shape.

Dorian Gray (The Picture of Dorian Gray 1890)

The only novel written by Oscar Wilde about the consequences of sin. It tells of a beautiful young man who trades his soul for beauty and youth. His sins are revealed in a portrait of him that betrays his corruption. It was first published in serial form by the Lippincott's Monthly Magazine in 1890 and then compiled into a book.

Dust Bowl (1934, 1936, 1939-1940)

The Dust Bowl occurred in the Great Plains of the United States when the top soil dried out and blew away causing gigantic dust clouds. This phenomenon was caused by drought and poor agricultural practices. Illnesses such as "dust pneumonia" result when humans and animals breathe in large quantities of dust, thus inflaming the alveoli and preventing the lungs from clearing. Symptoms include difficulty in breathing, chest pain, fever, and coughing. The Red Cross made and distributed dust masks during the Dust Bowl, but it is estimated 7000 people still died. Approximately, 3.5 million people migrated from the Midwest to other states where they could have a fresh state. These people were referred to as *Okies*. Read John Steinbeck's *Grapes of Wrath*.

Eleanor Roosevelt (1884-1962)

Served as First Lady of the United States from 1933 to 1945. During this time, Mrs. Roosevelt worked to expand the rights of working women, WWII refugees, and the civil rights of minorities. She advocated the U.S. join the United Nations and was appointed as its first delegate. Serving as first chair on the UN Commission on Human Rights, she oversaw the drafting of the Universal Declaration of Human Rights. Roosevelt later chaired President John Kennedy's Presidential Commission on the Status of Women. She was the niece of President Theodore Roosevelt and first cousin to Alice Roosevelt Longworth. Roosevelt married her fifth cousin once removed, Franklin Delano Roosevelt, who became the 32nd President of the U.S. She is considered one of the most admired people of the twentieth century.

Elevenses

An English custom of a break with refreshments about eleven o'clock before the lunch hour.

Gloria Vanderbilt (1924-2019)

An heiress of the Vanderbilt family. She was the niece of Viscountess Thelma Furness, who was mistress of the Prince of Wales, and mother to Anderson Cooper. Her aunt, Gertrude Vanderbilt Whitney, took Gloria's mother (Big Gloria) to court as an unfit mother for custody of Gloria (Little Gloria) in 1934. It created a stir coming on the heels of the Lindbergh baby kidnapping and murder. The aunt won the suit. Gloria grew up to become a designer and entrepreneur of upscale blue jeans and perfumes.

Great Depression (1929-1940)

A world-wide phenomenon caused by the U.S. stock market crash in October 1929. The years 1931-1934 were the worst years of the Depression with an unemployment percentage rate of 15.9, 23.6, 24.9, 21.7 respectively, and even in 1940 unemployment was fifteen percent. President FDR's New Deal programs such as the CCC and the WPA helped, but it wasn't until WWII that the country roared out of the Great Depression for good.

House of Saxe-Coburg and Gotha

A German dynasty founded by Ernest Anton, sixth duke of Saxe-Coburg-Saalfeld. In Great Britain, the Saxe-Coburgs were descendants of

(German) Albert, Prince Consort of (British) Queen Victoria (House of Hanover). In 1917, complaints about the British royal family's German surname caused King George V to change the name to the House of Windsor.

Joachim von Ribbentrop (1883-1946)

A German businessman who had many connections outside Germany and was considered an authority on foreign affairs by the Nazis. Like his American counterpart, William Donovan, who spied for the US, Ribbentrop collected information on his trips and reported back to the German government. A supporter of Nazi ideology, Ribbentrop offered his home as a location for secret meetings in January 1933 that resulted in Hitler's appointment as Chancellor of Germany. He was appointed as ambassador to Great Britain in 1936 and was rumored to have had an affair with Wallis Simpson, the paramour of Edward David Windsor, Prince of Wales. Before WWII, he was instrumental in negotiating an alliance with Fascist Italy (Pact of Steel) and the Nazi-Soviet non-aggression pact (Molotov-Ribbentrop Pact). After Japan's attack on Pearl Harbor, he supported Germany's declaration of war against the United States. In 1945, Ribben-trop was arrested, tried for war crimes at the Nuremberg trials due to helping to start WWII and facilitating the Holocaust. On October 16th, 1946, Ribbentrop was executed by hanging, along with other German WWII conspirators.

Jean Harlow (1911-1937)

Harlow was an American comedic actress and one of the first sex symbols of the "talkies." Known as the "Platinum Bombshell", she became one of Hollywood's biggest stars and is still ranked at No. 22 on AFI's greatest female stars of the Golden Age of Hollywood. Harlow died of kidney failure at the age of twenty-six.

Josiah Spode (1733-1797)

An English ceramicist who was famous for improving the formula for bone china by adding calcinated ox-bone in its formula—thus its name of *bone* china. This caused the china to be translucent when held up to the light. He is also recognized to have developed a technique for underglaze transfer printing. Spode china is very valuable.

Lancelot "Capability" Brown (1715-1783)

Known as one of England's great landscape gardeners, Brown's designs are influential to this day.

Mae West (1893-1980)

Miss West was an American stage and film actress who was arrested on moral charges for her play *SEX*. This notoriety made her a household name and Hollywood called for her. Although Miss West only made twelve films she is considered the 15th greatest female actress of the golden age of American cinema. Writing her own material for her films, West said, "I believe in censorship. I've made a fortune out of it." Her first film was *Night After Night* where a hatcheck girl says, "Goodness, what beautiful diamond," to which West replies, "Goodness had nothing to do with it, dearie." The star of the picture, George Raft, complained that West's appearance took the limelight off him. He said, "she stole everything but the cameras" meaning she appropriated his scenes with her brazen look, strutting walk, and comic delivery of her lines.

Mata Hari (1876-1917)

Hari was a Dutch exotic dancer who was executed by a French firing squad for spying for Germany during the Great War (WWI).

Mesopotamia

Name for the historical region between the Tigris-Euphrates river system. Also called the Fertile Crescent. Name covers the modern countries of Kuwait, Iraq, Syria, and Turkey. The area is now referred to as the Middle East which also includes Egypt, Sudan, Saudi Arabia, and other countries.

MI5 (Military Intelligence Section 5)

Founded in 1909 and specializing in domestic intelligence, it was originally a joint venture between the Admiralty and the War Office. While MI5 is a nickname, it was officially called Home Section of the Secret Service Bureau. MI6 specializes in foreign intelligence.

MI6 (Military Intelligence Section 6)

Also known as the Secret Intelligence Service (SIS) is the foreign intelligence service of the United Kingdom. Founded in 1909 as part of the

Secret Service Bureau, its duties expanded during WWI and adopted its current name in 1920. The SIS was not officially acknowledged until 1994 when the Intelligence Service Act of 1994 (ISA) was introduced to Parliament. And yes, like James Bond, MI6 agents do have a license to kill.

Mushy Peas
A British staple made from Marrowfat peas, which are larger and have a higher starch content than most pea offerings. Looks like thick pea soup. Mushy peas are eaten as a side dish or a "sauce" over other foods such as chips.

Nineteenth Amendment (Amendment XIX) to the US Constitution
The 19th amendment prohibits the states and the federal government from denying the right to vote to citizens of the United States on the basis of sex. It needed thirty-six states to pass the amendment, and Tennessee was the last state of the thirty-six to do so with only one vote passing it. Harry Burn, who was anti-suffrage for women, received a note from his mother, Phoebe Ensminger Burn, stating, "Hurrah, and vote for suffrage," and implored him to be a "good son."

Harry did what his mother wanted and cast the last vote for suffrage breaking the tie. The amendment was adopted in 1920 but was challenged by Leser v Garnett and Fairchild v Hughes. Some states refused to vote on the amendment while other states, mostly in the South, rejected it. States would reverse their rejection of the amendment in favor of it as late as 1984. One vote *can* make all the difference. Thank you, Mrs. Burn, for sending that note to your son.

Noel Coward (1899-1973)
Coward was an English playwright, actor, singer, composer, and director. He was considered one of the great wits of the 20th century and a noted letter writer. His most famous song is *Mad Dogs and Englishmen* and many of his plays were adapted to film. He is associated with Gertrude Lawrence and Marlene Dietrich.

Nowak
Polish surname that means "newcomer."

Oswald Mosley, 6th Baronet (1896-1980)
Mosley was the leader of the British Union of

Fascists (BUF). He was imprisoned in 1940 and the BUF was banned. He was released in 1943. Ruined and disgraced, Mosley was rejected for political office post WWII. He moved to France in 1951 for the remainder of his life.

Paul von Hindenburg (1847-1934)

A German general and war hero who led the German Army during the Great War (WW1). In 1925, he became President of the German Weimar Republic until his death in August of 1934. He was instrumental in the Nazi rise to power in Germany when he was forced to appoint Adolf Hitler as Chancellor of Germany. After Hindenburg died, Hitler combined the presidency and the chancellorship into one office with "führer" as the title for the new office. By September, Nazi control of Germany would be complete.

Pinkerton National Detective Agency

A private security firm created by Allan Pinkerton in the 1850s. The agency performed services ranging from security guarding to private military work. At the height of their power, they were hired by wealthy businessmen to infiltrate unions and intimidate workers. During the Homestead Strike of 1892, the Pinkertons confronted striking steel workers, causing the death of three Pinkertons and nine workers. The Pinkerton Agency is now a division of a Swedish company—Securitas AB.

Prince of Wales

Prince Edward Albert Christian George Andrew Patrick David, formally of the House of Saxe-Coburg and Gotha, now House of Windsor, was born in 1894 during the reign of his great-grandmother Queen Victoria to the Duke and Duchess of York. He was given the title of Prince of Wales on his sixteenth birthday. His father became George V in 1910 and when he died in 1936, the Prince of Wales became king taking the name Edward VIII. Within twelve months, he abdicated the throne in order to marry the American Wallis Simpson. Because she was twice-divorced, Simpson was considered socially and politically unacceptable as queen. They married in 1937 and self-exiled to France until David's death in 1972.

Savoy Hotel (1889-)
The Savoy was the first deluxe hotel in London boasting electric lights, elevators, and hot water. It was one of the first buildings in Great Britain to install air conditioning. This was the hotel of choice for aristocrats, the famous, and the nouveau rich.

SS Statendam 1934
A Holland-American passenger steamship whose route was New York to Rotterdam via Plymouth. The Commander of the ship was Captain J. J. Bijl. The ship has 1st, 2nd, and 3rd class accommodations.

Sicherheitsdienst (1931-1945)
An independent intelligence agency of the SS and the Nazi Party. It was considered a complementary organization to the Gestapo secret police. In 1939 it was mainlined into the Reich Security Main Office.

Trousers/Slacks
In the late 19th and early 20th century, women, riding bikes and enjoying other athletic activities, adopted a form of pants called bloomers or

knickerbockers. During WWI, women, working in factories and citing safety as a concern, threw off their dresses and wore pants but it was socially frowned upon. Three women were mainly responsible for American women wearing pants in the 1930s. German actress Marlene Dietrich's character in the 1930 film *Morocco*, was considered scandalous as she dressed in a tux and kissed a female audience member on the lips. First Lady, Eleanor Roosevelt wore trousers at the White House Easter Egg Roll in 1933. The woman who had the most influence on women wearing trousers was American actress Katharine Hepburn, who was the first woman to wear pants in a motion picture and was photographed wearing them in her private life. Wearing pants became socially acceptable when Rosie the Riveter, the iconic symbol of American women working in factories supporting the WWII effort, wore pants in her famous cover of the *Saturday Evening Post*.

Viscountess Thelma Furness (1904-1970)

Thelma Furness, Viscountess Furness, was the American mistress of the Prince of Wales until she was usurped by Wallis Simpson in 1934. She was a twin sister of Gloria Vanderbilt, the aunt of (Little) Gloria Vanderbilt, and the great-aunt of Anderson Cooper.

Wallis Simpson (1896-1986)

Simpson was an American socialite, who began an affair with Edward David Windsor, Prince of Wales, and heir to the British throne in 1934. After Wallis' divorce, her beau, now Edward VIII, King of United Kingdom, created a constitutional crisis when he announced his intention to marry the twice-divorced Mrs. Simpson. He abdicated the throne in 1936 in order to marry her. Both Simpson and the abdicated Edward VIII, now Duke of Windsor, were Nazi sympathizers and of great concern to the British government during WWII. The British went at great length to suppress intelligence from them. Prime Minister Winston Churchill even threatened the Duke if he did not follow orders from the British Government. Eventually, the Duke was appointed Governor of the Bahamas to get him and Simpson out of the Government's hair. After the war, the couple lived in France until their deaths. Simpson is attributed with the quote, "You can never be too rich or too thin."

Weimar Republic

Germany existed as a constitutional republic beginning in 1918 after the abdication of Kaiser Wilhelm and ended with President Paul Hindenburg's appointment of Adolf Hitler as chancellor in 1933. Thus Germany began its road to a dictatorship with the Nazis banning unions, other political parties, and a free press finally leading to WWII and genocide.

William Donovan (1883-1959)

An American soldier, lawyer, and intelligence officer, Donovan is the only veteran to receive all four of the United States highest awards—the Medal of Honor, the Distinguished Service Cross, the Distinguished Service Medal, and the National Security Medal plus the Silver Star and the Purple Heart. He is best known for serving as the head of the Office of Strategic Services (OSS) during WWII. Another famous alumnus of the OSS was French gourmet chef, Julia Child. The OSS evolved to become the Central Intelligence Agency (CIA) after 1945. Donovan was recruited by President Roosevelt in 1934 to "casually" collect information against Nazis living in the U.S. as the States did not have a formal protocol as spying was frowned upon. Secretary of State Henry L. Stimson, under President Hoover, wrote in his memoirs, "Gentlemen do not read each other's mail," and pulled funding for intelligence gathering. Roosevelt knew that Donovan was a loud critic of such action and felt the U.S. needed a formal intelligence department like the United Kingdom's MI6. As soon as the U.S. was attacked in 1941, Roosevelt demanded that he be granted money for such a department with Donovan heading it—thus began the OSS. Years later, Donovan died after developing dementia, taking all his secrets with him to the grave. A statue of Donovan stands in the CIA Headquarters lobby.

Winston Churchill (1874-1965)

Churchill was a British soldier, author, and statesman. Most notably known as Prime Minister of the United Kingdom during WWII and is credited with providing the leadership needed to save the country from defeat to the Nazis. He was a member of the Conservative Party. Churchill is credited with coining the term "Iron Curtain" in a speech about the USSR at Westminister College in Fulton, Missouri in 1946.

Yank
British slang for someone from the United States. Short for Yankee.

Books By Abigail Keam

Josiah Reynolds Mysteries

Mona Moon Mysteries

About The Author

Abigail Keam is an award-winning and Amazon best-selling author. She is a beekeeper, loves chocolate, and lives on a cliff overlooking the Kentucky River. Besides the *1930s Mona Moon Mysteries*, she writes the award-winning *Josiah Reynolds Mysteries*, *The Princess Maura Tales* (fantasy), and the *Last Chance For Love Series* (sweet romance).

Don't forget to leave a review! Tell your friends about Mona.

Thank you again, gentle reader, for your reviews and your word of mouth, which are so important for any book. I hope to meet you again between the pages.

CPSIA information can be obtained
at www.ICGtesting.com
Printed in the USA
LVHW101940181022
730978LV00002B/230